The Great Journey

The Great Journey

by

Jeffrey Jon Richards

Smithfield Press
North Richland Hills, Texas

Smithfield Press
An imprint of D. & F. Scott Publishing, Inc.
P.O. Box 821653
N. Richland Hills, TX 76182
817 788-2280
info@dfscott.com
www.dfscott.com

Copyright © 2002 by Jeffrey Jon Richards
All rights reserved.
No part of this book may be reproduced in any manner whatsoever without written permission of the publisher except for brief quotations embodied in critical articles or reviews.

Printed in the United States of America

06 05 04 03 02   5 4 3 2 1

ISBN 1-930566-24-7

Contents

Preface — vii

1 The Call — 1

2 March of Death — 27

3 Beginning of a Dream — 43

4 Connection — 63

5 Enemy Within — 93

6 The Trial — 115

About the Author — 130

Preface

As a product of both the North and South, my earliest recollections of racial issues mirrored remarkably varied views on the subject. I spent my first fifteen years in Minnesota, where the greatest ethnic controversy was whether one was either Norwegian, Swedish, or neither. But this was more of a family feud with generous heapings of humor. My mother's roots sprang from North Carolina, and during my formative years my family and I made an annual trek to the Tarheel state in order to visit relatives in the eastern section of the state. As a child, I became aware of the chasm between whites and blacks. Though occupying the same city physically, they were apparently light years apart in every other area of their lives. In comparison to the 1960s, racial issues in the fifties were, at least outwardly, years of resignation on the part of blacks and contentment on behalf of whites. But the underlying animosities by the mid sixties would erupt from their seething cauldron.

Since that decade, there has been a fairly predictable ebb and flow concerning black and white relations. Many whites remind me of an ostrich with its head in the sand, saying something to the effect that they cannot see that there is a problem. Of course, white supremacist groups continue to propagate hatred between the races. For many whites, racial issues are only an annoyance; the reasoning is that there are far weightier issues in which to be engaged. For the majority of black Americans, daily life is viewed as a constant struggle revolving around the perennial issue of perceived racism. There are not many like George Foreman, Michael Jordon, Oprah Winfrey, and Dianna Ross who not only have done

Preface

well financially, but also have captured the hearts of most; they seem to have transcended the color issue.

The majority of the characters in *The Great Journey* are fictional; however, most of those associated with Martin Luther King, Jr. are historical. The events leading up to King's assassination are based upon historical record. Though the plot is fictional, I believe that the reader will perceive that the book has a realistic tone especially as seen in the two main characters, Angus Clark and Thomas Jackson.

The two ministers, one black and the other white, fuse into a symbol—that of the evergreen possibility of racial reconciliation. As pastors of two of America's mega-churches, their ministries wield a great impact, not only on matters religious, but on cultural issues as well. However, there is a force which will not rest until all that they stand for is destroyed—Ray Rubens and the United Invisible Empire. As a resurrected and strengthened hate group composed of Neo-Nazis, women's hate groups, and the old Ku Klux Klan, the newly formed movement is determined to destroy any semblance of multiculturalism and harmony among the races.

Along with the two ministers, Terrence Brown, a Harvard Law School graduate, one-time, fictional confidant of Martin Luther King, Jr., and ex Green Beret, is a key player in the plot which spans from the 1950s to the year 2003. As president of the Coalition of Black People, he is convinced that he and his movement can bring justice for all races in America, even if force is needed. Though he is brilliant, the book documents Brown's personal awareness that there is much in life which reason cannot explain and also that there may be something which is greater than hate.

Angus Clark and Thomas Jackson become the two leaders of a growing national reconciliation movement which even gains the full support of the president of the United States

Preface

and several key congressional senators. But it is not long before Ray Rubens and the United Invisible Empire are able to seemingly crush the movement. But payday is coming for Ray Rubens.

I do not believe that it is an overstatement to say that racial issues are one of the primary concerns today. Multiculturalism has somewhat taken the focus off of the historic black and white struggle, but it appears to me still to be the dominant form of racism in America. Many blacks continue to speak about the reality of the "glass ceiling" and other forms of harassment. The subject of black and white relations continues to be a cutting-edge topic; in a sense this form of racism forms the paradigm for all others. While some are intrigued with variety, for many, different actually means danger and threat. Recently, several newspaper articles and television documentaries have been devoted to the issues of who really killed Martin Luther King, Jr. as well as various forms of racism.

Politicians, reformers, activists, and educators continue to discuss the issue and in many instances have accomplished some lasting good. But the fact remains that there is no lasting earthly or human solution on the near or remote horizon.

This book is an attempt to understand the conflict. Perhaps like me, Americans are discovering that they are interacting with those of other races more so now than at any other time in their lives; whether or not the United States will be truly united depends ultimately upon each one of us.

Jeffrey Jon Richards
Salisbury, North Carolina
Spring 2002

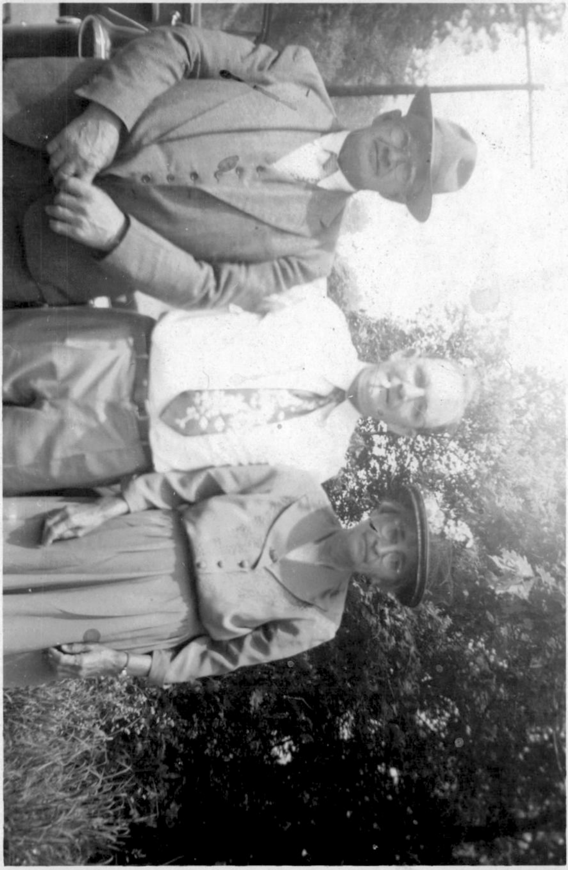

1

The Call

The two ministers had been through harrowing experiences during the past several years. Angus Clark inquired of his friend, "Did we do the right thing by not taking the law into our own hands?"

"We did the best we could under the circumstances. And wasn't it you who shouted to Terrence, 'Let the highest court take care of him'?"

"Thomas, it does not matter if Ray Rubens is ever seen again; he has set in motion by clever, diabolical design, a civil war which unlike the first one will never unite this country."

The taut faces mirrored their tenseness about the situation. They both rose slowly from kneeling in prayer at the altar on that sweltering Saturday in July 2003 in the Ebenezer Baptist Church in Charlotte, North Carolina; the tranquillity of the atmosphere of the four-thousand seat sanctuary could not erase their anguish over the racial war in their city.

"Angus," inquired his friend Thomas, "looking at that cross before us shows how something so precious can be warped and twisted. How is it possible for that ultimate symbol of life and hope to be used by some to mean death and destruction?"

"Without doubt there has been evil, creative license concerning the symbol of the cross. Look again at the swastika. Every

The Great Journey

time that I see it, I am reminded of concentration camps and the extermination of millions by a few evil people."

Their very souls and emotions felt contorted. Both were numb with anxiety as they understood that the portents of destruction ominously loomed over the country. Each inquired of the other if he believed that God had heard their prayers.

The question of how it had ever happened became the silent cry between them. The war was not only in Charlotte, but was also occurring in every major metropolitan area in America. It was obvious that the recent escalating events were the result of careful and precision planning. Angus long remembered the words of a black minister who years before had declared with prophetic conviction, "Racism is the worst sin in America." The two ministers' prayers had been for reconciliation of the racial riots that had been tearing at the city for three months, and they wondered how matters had gone from tense to insane in so short a period of time. The media, of course, had been incessant in its portrayal of the conflict with never-ending images of fights, window smashing, looting, and especially killings. There was speculation that matters would only become worse even though the president of the United States had made special appeals and continued to make impassioned speeches personally in several large cities; but still the battles continued in spite of military involvement. There was no denying America was trapped in the gripping vice of the results of centuries of racism. There was talk that this would be America's second revolution; the first being for independence over two hundred years ago, but this one for true equality between the two major races which built America.

The Call

Though brewing below the surface for decades, trouble emerged in 1998. The Klan decided after several years of solitude to make its presence known.

Tommy Johns was just plain trouble. He had been married three times, and now was seeing several women. He never had steady work but managed to keep body and soul together by working at various odd jobs. He usually had alcohol breath, typically the whiskey kind. As a teenager, he had been charged with second-degree murder but through some odd coincidence was never convicted. The verdict was "there is not enough solid evidence," so he was able to walk. His greatest asset, some said, was his loud mouth and his ability to bark out orders. An only child, he only faintly remembered his mother and father. He was only four years old when he witnessed two black men intrude into his house and steal, not only some cash, but the lives of his parents. Recurring nightmares of the repeated stabbings of those two people who could never be replaced were common. The murderers hadn't seen Tommy, nor were they ever found.

"Let it burn good and long, Tommy Johns!" shrieked one of the ten Klansmen on that chilly, dark November 1998 evening.

"This uppity nigger has been saying too much for too long now, and it's time that he learns he ain't gonna speak any longer 'gainst us," bellowed out another half-inebriated, robe-clad, heavy-set young man.

"Tommy, should we burn this dump? It shouldn't take too long, not as long as it is taking that cross to burn," another excitedly inquired from within the pack.

"No, let's just get out of here; we might be far out in the country, but there may be some others like Brown, or some white nigger lovers roaming about, and that would be just plain trouble," retorted their leader. The drunken klansmen laughed as they drank in what they were doing to Brown's land. It was an eerie night. Not too far away, several barred owls had been identifying their territory, only to accentuate the forlornness of the night.

The twisting, narrow road leading to and from Terrence Brown's small farm was filled with ruts; he lived out in the county, at least five miles from any gas station or grocery store. He had inherited the fifty acres from his father, who had been the son of a sharecropper. The memories of childhood included the backbreaking manual harvesting of both cotton and tobacco. Their farm "machinery" consisted of several stubborn mules, which Terrence often would ride, pretending that he was mounted on a Kentucky thoroughbred. Usually, they attempted to engage in their own veterinary work for the mules which always seemed to be coming down with various illnesses. But a few times his father, and even he himself, employed the services of veterinarians, in particular Dr. Garfield Clark. Angus Clark, as a child, had accompanied his father to the Brown's on at least three occasions, and he and Terrence amused themselves by attempting to ride a couple of the mules. That was many years ago, but soon they would meet again.

Terrence's father had been hanged by a dozen Klansmen back in 1962. He had been very outspoken concerning their terrorizing some of the local residents, and finally several members of the Klan decided that they had had enough of him. Terrence and his brothers and sisters were not home at the time; the lifeless, dangling, bruised body was discovered by their mother on that dreadful May morning. Like the song "Patches," Terrence, at a very early age, found himself as the primary caretaker for much of the hard work around the farm. But he had shouldered the responsibility with great encouragement from his mother and two younger sisters and brothers. Somehow he managed to maintain enormous courage as he became the man of the household.

The Call

Blessed with a superior mind, he consistently was at the top of his classes during his teenage years.

The Klansmen were there the night of the cross burning at Brown's because reliable sources had informed them that Terrence would not be around for a few days. It was known that Terrence kept several pistols and rifles; he was a crack shot. He had also been a Green Beret who had seen considerable action during the last years of the Vietnam War. The Klansmen that night had little knowledge of his background and his many other associations. They were only following orders.

The Klansmen stood motionless for about a minute longer, viewing what they believed to be a sacred sight. Throughout the many decades of the Klan's growing influence, most Christians viewed the burning of the cross as nothing short of sacrilege, that is, the desecration of its most sacred symbol of redemption and hope. For many, the cross's sacredness was related to the fact that Jesus' death was for all of humanity and that through a personal acceptance of the Christ of the cross, one might be ultimately reconciled to God and united with Him. Being right with God, it was then possible to be united with all human beings, no matter what their heritage. But for a true Klansman, this was meaningless theology.

Suddenly, a high powered gunshot rang out, shattering any conjured notion of tranquillity. Tommy Johns in anguish cried out as he was thrown to the hard red clay earth, "I've been shot!"

"Where are our guns?" anxiously yelled another. The rapid gunfire continued until two more Klansmen were hit; both were shot in the lower legs. Almost as quickly as it had begun, the gunfire stopped. The ten somehow managed to jump or crawl into the cab or back of the Confederate-flag-decorated

The Great Journey

pickup, and make their way out of the darkness silhouetted by the lone-burning cross.

As they raced over the bumpy road, with fiendish anger one of the ten bellowed, "I thought you said that the boy was not home."

Billy Boggs excitedly exclaimed, "Whoever that guy is, he knows how to shoot. It was like he knew exactly where to place the next shot. I've never seen such calm and fancy shooting."

Another added, "Let's get our guns and go back and finish him off!"

"The way he can shoot, you're crazy," shouted Billy. "He will easily place his next shots in someone's brain."

Through words of anguishing pain, Tommy convinced them to forget any such thoughts, and to just get where they had planned to go. No one's wounds were life threatening, although it appeared that Tommy's left arm had been broken, and he was bleeding profusely. One of the men used his cell phone and reached the house of their destination. The lady of the home was instructed to call a local M.D. who was sympathetic to the cause. They were assured that he would not divulge any of the night's events.

After driving for over an hour, the group found themselves in Mayfield, a small town located about fifty miles south of Raleigh. The Grand Dragon of the Southeastern Chapter of the KKK, Ray Rubens, was hosting an all night rally in his large, immaculate home, and he was especially anxious to hear about the most recent ventures of his "children," as he delighted in calling those who belonged to his chapter. Tales about Rubens were legendary, some going as far back as thirty years. The rumor was that he had a 30-30 mounted in a rifle jacket on the driver's side door of his glistening, late model, white Lincoln town car. Though no white man or

The Call

woman had officially testified against him in any court of law, common rumor, especially among law enforcement officers and judges, was that he had been involved in vandalism, burning of homes and places of business, extensive theft of many black-owned companies, and several brutal murders of blacks and Jews. A few leading Roman Catholics were also the subjects of his scathing verbal attacks.

Rubens was tall and lanky; his face had that hard, leathery look of one who had spent a great deal of time in the outdoors. His long gray hair made him look older than his fifty-five years. He had some peculiar mannerisms such as raising his head higher when in conversation. That characteristic made some feel as if he were censoring them. Clean-shaven, one might wonder why he did not grow a goatee to cover up the very obvious scar which crisscrossed his lower chin. His strong mountain accent betrayed him as one who was raised in the western section of the state. In fact, he had lived for many years west of Asheville, very close to the Tennessee border. Though he had not attended college, his keen intelligence was at once obvious. He spoke deliberately; one always had the impression that he was weighing the effect of each one of his syllables. He spurned others if they used a calculator since he never did so, but effortlessly added long columns of numbers without the aid of any instrumentation. A person who paid attention to details, he kept copious records, although his memory would have been sufficient. Surprisingly, he could be a person who was quick with a joke, but usually such jesting was at the expense of the other person, and certainly never himself. Though he had an intimidating demeanor about him, he elicited great respect from his "children," although some were known to liken such respect more to fear, such as the fear of God. A wealthy man, he was able to dispense very grand gifts to those who pleased him with their deeds. It was not known how he had acquired such an amount of wealth and real estate because he was not the kind of person to divulge such information.

The Great Journey

Several women were there that night; most were the wives of Rubens's "children." An outsider might be somewhat taken back at how wholesome and personable most of them were, especially one named Ginger. The Grand Dragon's home was opulent. Several marble columns lined the large banquet hall. The temperature of the water of the indoor swimming pool was always a little on the chilly side, just the way Rubens liked it. For those who had seen *Gone with the Wind*, the winding stairs seemed especially familiar. The house was complete with several secret rooms and two long underground passageways, just in case a hurried escape was necessary. Some thought it odd that he had a special room which housed crypts where the remains of several key Klansmen were kept.

It was Ginger who took the call from the ten who were scheduled to meet with Ray Rubens. She was both alarmed and relieved since her husband was not one of the three who had been wounded. She kept the phone conversation continuing for a lengthy time, but then reminded her husband that she must immediately call the doctor. About forty minutes later, the truck pulled into the impressive-looking circular drive, and the wounded were cared for immediately.

Later, those who were able gathered around the leader. "Well boys, I certainly don't have to ask you how things went tonight!"

One named Jimmy whimpered, "Boss, we had no idea the creep was home when we had that cross burning; it was a beautiful sight! We thought we would be able to enjoy our work for a long time. We even thought about burning his house, but then he started shooting. If only we had left sooner. Better yet, if only we hadn't gone!"

"Everything is so much simpler in retrospect," replied Rubens ruefully. "We can all be thankful no one was killed."

The Call

Another Klansman somewhat defensively inquired, "Boss, what was so important that we go to a shack and burn a cross? I mean it's not like this guy is a heavyweight or anything!"

"Oh really!" hissed Rubens. "Let me tell you about this Terrence Brown. He was with Martin Luther King in Memphis. Because of his prowess as a Green Beret, King had especially wanted Brown to accompany him, mainly as a bodyguard. But King also thought Brown had the qualities to one day take over for him, or at least be a key figure in the inner circle and continue the revolution."

"Boss, you didn't tell us all this!" The twenty-two people who filled the room listened in rapt attention as Rubens continued.

"He is also the only one," continued Rubens, "who knew and fingered one of our own as the assassin of King—James Earl Ray! The conclave of Grand Dragons has kept this under wraps for years; we never wanted anyone to know, even members of the Klan. As you remember, we had informed you over the years that Ray was not the killer, and that we did not know who was. But now that Ray is dead, and so many years have passed, we have decided it's OK if the information gets out. Eventually, we will get Brown; we thought tonight would be good just as a reminder, kind of like leaving our calling card. But obviously this time it did not turn out as we hoped. For some time now, I have been receiving reliable information that Brown is bent on stirring up trouble among his own people. Seems that he has been doing a good deal of speaking in black churches, large ones especially, and even some white ones. We have been told he also has been conducting some secret anti-Klan rallies. We had to get rid of his father more than thirty-five years ago, and it looks like we will have to do the same with his son. Inside word is that he has been working with an influential black preacher in Charlotte; his name escapes me at the moment. What is that name?" He stared for sometime as if in a trance. "Oh, yes, that's the pastor of that large Ebenezer Church in north Charlotte, the Rev. Thomas Jackson."

The conversation at Rubins's house that night centered on the explosive information which they had learned from their leader. Their motive was indeed retaliation, even though most agreed, it was also to stem what they knew Brown was capable of, especially when combined with the efforts of one of the most influential black preachers, if not of all preachers, in America. They somehow instinctively sensed that the Brown/Jackson duo would mean huge problems for the Klan. They had to be stopped.

He was a respected leader in community matters as well as in the church. He had a demeanor about him which instantly commanded attention. If one were to sum up Angus Clark in a word, it would be "character." His parents had instilled in him at an early age a strong work ethic, but this was balanced with a strong sense of compassion for others—especially those who were less fortunate. As senior pastor of Charlotte's New Covenant Church, one of the largest Presbyterian churches in America, his ministry was widely known. In particular, it was his style and content of preaching, nationally broadcast on both radio and television, that made him so popular. His ministry also had cutting-edge technology which utilized the latest trends on the net. But recently he had abandoned his typical format, and unlike many within his denomination, he began to speak out boldly against racism. He knew that he was involving himself in a controversial issue, the outcome of which could lead to either heaven or hell on earth. Most white ministers in the city, as well as those across the country, were still under the conviction that racial issues were best left ignored.

The Call

Concluding his third sermon for the morning on that second Sunday in July 1999, he forcefully articulated, "The Lord would have us all express compassion, love, and justice to all. Knowing that God loves each one of us with a love which is unfathomable, so must each of us express this kind of love especially to those who are of another race." He was preaching a series on racial reconciliation, basing his messages on select passages from both the Old and New Testaments. At first he found the study tedious, and he began to wonder if he had entered into water which might be too deep for him. Only two years ago, Angus had had no interest in the issue. After all, he was a product of the South, and his early environment, which had advocated tolerance at best and antagonism at worst, had subtly found its way into his psyche. More tolerant than most, he had not seen the issue as deserving of his fullest efforts. Oh yes, he had been moved by King's "I Have a Dream Speech"; even his reading of *Black Like Me* had stirred him, at least for the moment, but that had been the extent of his involvement or even his thought concerning the subject. The seminary from which he graduated, though not located in the South, fostered the same attitude. The very few who were of other races were primarily from Asian countries or India; there were only two blacks in the entire seminary. Most blacks felt unwelcome and therefore preferred their own institutions.

But through reading the Bible, other various books, and ultimately in pleading with God to reveal what his attitude should be concerning the continuing potentially explosive topic of racial issues, he gradually found himself aware of the importance of the subject. He was, of course, knowledgeable of the major racial topic in the New Testament, which was the racial antagonism between the Samaritans and the Jews. But after further study, he was able to see that indeed the main characters in both testaments had considerable interaction among various ethnic groups. In fact, Israel is located close to northeast Africa as well as to Iraq and Iran, and throughout both the Old and New Testaments, one finds repeated references to key characters and countries representing a variety of ethnic groups, including many which are black. He had been aware of the repeated mention of Ethiopia and Egypt especially in the Old Testament. For some reason, though, the issue of ethnicity had escaped his concern, and he had continued with the usual mistake of interpreting the Bible as if it were a book that was not composed and compiled in the Middle East—a melting pot of cultures and ethnic groups.

His study of the book of Genesis, especially chapters 1 and 2, created in him a new interest in the phrase "the image of God." As he read about humanity created in God's image, he concluded that all peoples had this blessing, and not just a select few. He had read all of the conclusions concerning this image, and he himself, after much study, believed that the image was something spiritual. It had something to do with the capacity to use one's mind, to make rational choices, and to express one's unique individual self. He finally concluded that to be prejudiced against any person based upon ethnic reasons was totally against God's way of relating to human beings. He sometimes humorously wondered if most Christians—American Protestants, Catholics, and Orthodox, had ever fully realized that Jesus was born Jewish; that more than likely, he had a dark complexion, dark eyes, and coarse, dark hair. Over the years, as Angus had viewed the typical caricature of Jesus, he saw a very Anglo-Saxon-looking Jesus, complete with blue eyes and a light hair color. He wondered if the phrase "Seeing is believing" should not at times be changed to "Believing is seeing," especially in this case. Sometimes he found himself tempted to remind people of this, but he rarely did as he was usually afraid of insulting people's intelligence by giving insight into the obvious.

There were just seven more days before Christmas, 1998, and the monthly meeting of the Board of New Covenant

The Call

Presbyterian Church was going smoothly. The Board was comprised of forty-seven men and women, most of whom were respected community leaders. One of the elders, a white man in his late thirties named Thad Cornelius exclaimed angrily, "Dr. Clark, obviously we appreciate you and your ministry here. You have brought national and even international attention to this church. But now many are saying that you have taken this racial thing too far! I remember that my daddy used to say people like you, have 'niggeritis,' and now I think I know what he was talking about. The papers and media are twisting what you are saying, and keep in mind that our television audience is also a huge supporter of this ministry. It appears that you are doing more harm than good. You are actually hindering the church's image. Instead of a refuge which provides peace, security, and love, especially for our members, we are now viewed as this kind of radical, right wing, in-your-face, down-with-tradition, multi-cultural, holy huddle. Pastor, why have you allowed this to happen? Don't talk to us about the thousands of new people who are coming, your ridiculous building program, and all this national attention. The fact is our faithful members are not getting their needs met. Instead they have a pastor who thinks he is some kind of media prima donna. My roots in this church go back for generations; my grandfather was even an elder here. But I can honestly say that I do not want my children and grandchildren to be part of this mess! If my granddaddy could see what is going on at this church now, he would roll over in his grave. Furthermore, we have been hearing reports that not only have you been attending some black churches, but you have actually been speaking from their pulpits! If we had wanted a black pastor, we would have gotten one. Imagine, we have a pastor who preaches in a black pulpit, and then comes to ours as if he has been left untainted. Also, the women are upset especially with your wife because she apparently supports you in these activities, and she has been seen attending some of these black church activities. May I remind you, you did all these dealings without getting our permission."

"Mr. Cornelius," Angus stated directly and confidently, "I am surprised that you have so misread the motives of this ministry. Remember, that the entire board voted its approval of this series against racism. I have been most aware through the weeks that some members have been upset. It certainly would have been easier for me not to have become involved in preaching about this subject. Change is always difficult, and while I respect tradition, in some cases there comes a point when traditions and the business-as-usual mentality have to go, and on this issue, this is where I stand."

The tension was mounting like mercury in a thermometer on a scorching summer day. The discussion continued back and forth with several other members heatedly voicing their opinions. The majority of the board members appeared to side with Angus Clark, but there were several influential members who strongly disagreed. Angus found himself once again in an antagonistic confrontation with Thad Cornelius whose face was becoming redder by the second. A big man, Cornelius rose from his chair, which was on the opposite side of the long boardroom table; snorting words of vindication, he rushed to the opposite end of the table and demanded Angus stand up and apologize to him. The pastor, who had taken great care not to offend anyone, offered some calming words, but clearly stated that he was going to hold to his position on the matter.

"You think that you are God!" screamed Thad Cornelius, who at the same time hit Angus with a crushing right fisted blow, sending him sprawling across the boardroom table, scattering tall drinking glasses, notebooks, and several people. Dazed, Angus regained his senses, but instead of cowering off, he lunged at the larger man knocking both of them off their feet. For some time they wrestled with each other,

The Call

intermittently exchanging heavy blows. Meanwhile, several of the other members of the board who had been at odds with one another, began verbally and in some cases physically abusing each other. Even some of the women were caught up in the fracas.

The mayhem lasted for several minutes until someone with a booming voice cried out, "In the name of God, what is going on here? Are we attempting to destroy not only ourselves, but also the work of God? How can we lead others if we ourselves are such poor examples?" The room fell silent. It was as if everyone awoke from a nightmare—chairs and papers were strewn about. Water was spilled; a few people stood in huddles gaping at those who had been involved in the fray. Finally, all sat down at the large table, and almost instinctively there was an attempt to bring order out of chaos. Apologies were very gradually uttered, phrases such as "I lost control," and "How stupid of me," were heard for the next hour. Other than a few ripped shirts and blouses, smeared makeup, a couple of ties which looked like they could never be worn again, one or two bloody noses, swollen lips, black eyes, and a couple of wigs which were not quite positioned as they should be, no one was permanently physically hurt. But all had a whole new awareness of the explosive nature of racial issues. If this topic could turn that boardroom filled with supposedly staid, dignified Christian individuals into a mini-war zone, Angus wondered with trepidation, what would happen out there, beyond the walls of their place of refuge in Charlotte.

It had been several weeks since the Klan's episode at Terrence Brown's. The incident had been the major topic of conversation for those who were Ray Rubens's "children." No plans had been formulated as of yet, but there had been several sug-

The Great Journey

gestions ranging from burning his house down to murder. Somehow the events of the episode had leaked to the local press, a fact which infuriated the local Klan members, especially the Grand Dragon. There was a great deal of talk about another march, this time in Charlotte, but it was decided that the timing was not right. On this night, once again at Rubens's, three Klansmen were presenting to a group of over seventy people what they had discovered about Terrence Brown.

After their briefings, Rubens gave further substantial information. "Ladies and Gentlemen, my children," he grandiosely announced, "we have some interesting information to tell you about Terrence Brown. Several of my lieutenants have spent considerable time gathering reliable information concerning this threat not only to our security, but to the continuation of the time-honored KKK.

Brown has managed to fool many over the years into believing that he is this poor, ignorant, debt-threatened farmer barely scraping by, but he is, as he has always been, a master of deception. The fact is that he is very rich and powerful. It seems that after King's assassination in Memphis, Brown went to law school at Harvard, graduating in the top 10 percent of his class. After graduation, he received various offers from several prestigious law firms, but he chose instead to be inducted into the NAACP, where he steadily climbed up the ranks into their inner circle. He now holds a key position from which the president of the organization is usually tapped. Not only is he a leader in this organization, but he is also highly influential in the Southern Christian Leadership Conference, the SCLC. It is primarily because of him that these two organizations work in tandem with each other. With the fusing of these two organizations, blacks are in a position to present a great threat to all of white America. We know he is able to influence some of the justices on the Supreme Court. We even have reports that he will pick up where Jesse Jackson left off concerning a run for the presidency in 2004. Also, because so many black pastors are

The Call

heavily involved in politics, he has been influencing a substantial number, including Thomas Jackson who is the pastor of that huge black Ebenezer Church in Charlotte. Yes, boys, had we known the full story of Terrence Brown, we would have certainly finished him off a long time ago. We thought his story had ended with King, but it is obvious that this fiend is thriving, and he and his ilk must be stopped."

"So, boss, why does he live in that dump?" inquired one very thoroughly confused Klansman.

"That is obviously a cover for him, and I might add, one that is quite clever. Of course, we know that he has other homes, at least one in the Caribbean Islands, another in L.A., and yet another in New Jersey, right across the river from the city. He uses several aliases and is most able in his use of disguises. One of them is very interesting—word is that he has a most convincing white man disguise."

"Now that is one that I would love to see," jeered Ginger mockingly.

After more extended conversation, Rubens closed, "We will need to meet within a month to come to some conclusions concerning all that has been discussed tonight. Everyone needs to continue to be vigilant."

Shortly after this meeting, an important conversation occurred.

"Thomas, this is Martin," stated the cultured voice. "I thought it was time that we chat since it has been several months."

"Hey, good to hear again from you, my friend. We just do not have the chance to speak to one another as much as in the past. I tried your last e-mail address, but apparently you have changed that recently."

"Yeah, I have had to change my server several times. I think my messages were being too closely monitored, if you know what I mean."

Thomas cautioned, "Oh, yes, in fact there is a good chance that we have unwelcome listeners at the moment."

Martin continued, "We will just have to use our usual coded language; I doubt if there are many, if any, who can quite figure out what we are saying."

Martin Luther King III was the oldest child of Dr. King. Unlike his father, he had not entered the ministry, but became heavily involved in politics. He was one of the key leaders of the SCLC and also was highly influential in the NAACP. A natural leader, he believed he could help the cause of racial equality better as a layperson rather than as a clergyman. Now approaching middle age, he still recalled vividly the news of the death of his father. He had been emotionally close to him, though his father's schedule did not permit him to spend the amount of time with his father he had desired. For several years, he had felt rage toward James Earl Ray; he viewed him as the epitome of "poor white trash." But as he studied Ray and read the psychological reports and began to understand his emotional make-up, he found himself gradually developing a curious, but genuine pity for the man. He became convinced that James Earl Ray was not the man who had killed his father; there were just too many inconsistencies. Besides, he had repeatedly received solid information of the Klan's involvement. Though Thomas Jackson was eight years older than he, the two had forged a strong friendship, born out of mutual struggle and the conviction that there is a God who cares and watches over the mockeries of justice. Martin recalled the many ser-

The Call

mons of his father preached with great Baptist fervor, and how the major theme was God's love and justice for all human beings. But mostly, he remembered a father who loved him deeply.

"Thomas, the reason I am calling you is to set up a time in which you can meet with me and Terrence Brown. I don't know if you have heard about it or not, but about a month ago, Terrence had a cross burned in front of one of his houses, not the one in either New Jersey or L.A., but his bungalow outside of Fayetteville. There were about a dozen Klansmen there, and well, finally Terrence said that he said to himself, 'Why should I take any more of this junk,' and he started shooting. A couple or more klansmen were shot. He claimed that he had genuinely feared for his life, since he was not sure just what kinds of ammo they had with them. He told me that he could just imagine flame throwers, dynamite, and assault weapons being used on him. But he said it was the strangest sight to see them crawling and scrambling to their pickup and speeding out of there. He believed, and maybe not so jokingly, that there must have been a gathering of angels around his house that only the Klan members could see. He even claimed that one reason he only told a couple of people is because no one would believe it!"

"Was anyone killed?" Thomas asked excitedly.

"No, thank the Lord. You know Terrence has always had this thing about 'not taking any guff,' and thank God, he wasn't firing too well that night, or so he said. We both know that he is an expert shot, and he spared all their lives that night."

"Why didn't we hear anything about this?" quizzed Thomas.

"Oh, you know the Klan; they are specialists in keeping events out of the news. Besides, they probably have a lot of influence with the papers and the rest of the media. Word is

The Great Journey

that several K sympathizers make sure the public only reads and hears what they want anyway."

"Thomas," continued Martin, "let's meet at the Renaissance in Charlotte on October 8, at 7:30 p.m. Terrence has already said the date and time suits him."

"OK, but I'm still not sure what all the agenda entails."

King continued, "There are many unsettled issues within the NAACP as well as the SCLC, and as leaders in both organizations, we need to set the pace. Also, there is so much talk about this racial war thing; in fact, there are many who are saying that everything is in place for war to start soon. There are radical cores within both groups advocating revolution. They are basically saying that the glass ceiling is continuing, and that it will only get worse. Some are advocating action groups in every major metropolitan area in the country..."

Thomas interjected, "We had better not discuss this anymore on the phone. I'll see you in Charlotte."

It had been two weeks since the tussle at New Covenant, and though profuse apologies had been offered, Angus believed that none of the issues had been resolved. There were strong words said against him, and he knew that much of it was in anger. The volume and intensity of the tirade by Thad Cornelius culminating in the slugfest, caused him to deeply doubt whether he should continue in his ministry. Yes, he had been blessed beyond anything he or perhaps anyone else could have imagined. He, with the help of the Lord, certainly had built one of the top five influential churches in the nation; it was not uncommon for U.S. senators to drop in every now and then. President Bush had attended one of his services in the early 1990s—an event that Angus would never forget.

The Call

Billy Graham had recently preached there as well as younger well-known evangelists and Christian leaders.

He found himself involved in intense, in-depth soul searching, pleading with the Lord to show him what part was his responsibility. At one point, he was willing to admit that it was all his fault, but then he remembered that his calling was unlike that of any other. He came to realize that he was involved in a great spiritual battle, similar to a physical war with high-powered weaponry. The enemy was invisible, and the weapons used against him were spiritual. Angus's personal conversion experience meant he belonged to God, and since he did, he reasoned that it was logical that there would be spiritual opposition from the other side—sometimes coming in the form of those who were even within the supposed fold. As this conclusion gradually dawned on him, it gave him added strength and the resolve to continue. Of course, the support of Sarah, his wife, and the positive vote of the Board, even with its handful of dissenters, added more resolution to his cause.

Angus remembered his studies of church history and theology in particular, which were foundational to his understanding and practice of ministry. He came away from the study of such subjects with the awareness that ultimately God is the Lord of history, its movements, and even the setting up and deposing of key historical figures. His personal theology held to the reality of evil, and that ultimately evil serves the very purpose of God. Somehow he was able to conclude that such atrocities as the Holocaust and Jonestown, along with truly evil people such as Nero and Hitler, somehow serve God's ultimate purpose. His theology professors as well as the doctrinal position of the seminary and the denomination which ordained him, believed in the reality of sin. That is, sin is not a lack of self-awareness or ignorance, but it is a tangible principle which finds its mark in every individual, and that some are more adept at expressing this inclination than others. He believed

The Great Journey

that all the evil in the world, including his personal experience of not always living as he believed that the Lord desired, was an expression of this thing called "sin."

He had a strong belief in angels, both beneficent and evil, but he rarely dwelt on the subject since he was somewhat fearful that others might deem that he was attempting to sensationalize a topic which ultimately is not verifiable. Nevertheless, he was convinced that God had on several occasions dispensed perhaps innumerable angels to come to his and others' aid. He not so jokingly shared with Sarah that he thought the devil or at least some of his demons were present in the boardroom during that event two weeks ago. Angus probably would be described by other pastors and theologians as one who was "biblical," that is, he took the Bible not only seriously, but on the whole literally. He usually punctuated his sermons and talks with phrases such as "according to the Scriptures," or "the Bible says." Rarely did he back up a point by saying something such as, "this is my feeling on the issue," or quote some well-known theologians to justify his own beliefs. Not that he had a disrespect for academia; after all, he was a graduate of some of the best schools in the country, and he had even earned a doctorate in theology. He firmly held to the conviction that his calling was so unlike any other, that at times he would come to an impasse. He would ultimately be cast upon faith and not reason, and there would continue to be issues which would defy reason and intellect altogether. More than two decades in ministry had shown him repeatedly his ultimate reliance upon the God who has revealed himself in the Word, the Old and New Testaments of the Bible. Some of the other pastors and theologians not only in North Carolina, but around the U.S. and even internationally, were critical of his theological and biblical views with comments such as "he is such a literalist," or "all he talks about is the Bible." Angus was aware that such hyperboles were in a sense backhanded compliments, for they indicated people were listening to him Many even took him seriously.

The Call

Al Bartelli, a U.S. senator from New Jersey, was one of Angus's closest friends; they had maintained their friendship since their days at Davidson, where both were baseball players. The call was routed to Angus by Diane Johnson, his personal secretary. "Angus, how are you doing these days?" inquired the senator with kindly affection. "It's been way too long since we have gotten together for lunch or a game of golf. How'd you like to hit a few this afternoon, say beginning at 2:00?"

It was at the ninth hole that Angus inquired, "Al, you seem to have more on your mind today than hitting the ball, not to be critical, but I have seen you play a whole lot better, my friend. I'm sure that you have played since our last game about three months ago."

Al stopped in the middle of his swing. He gazed at Angus—long enough to let him know that something was weighing heavily upon him and that he had something important to say.

"I have been working with the CIA recently, Angus."

"Don't tell me that you have finally discovered what is going on at New Covenant," Angus said jokingly. The jocular banter between them was something that they enjoyed.

"The issue concerns one of your colleagues in ministry, Thomas Jackson. I have heard you speak of him favorably here in the past year or so, and I know that your friendship goes back to the sixties though there was a long hiatus of three decades when you two were in separate parts of the country. Well, we have been receiving some disturbing reports recently. It seems that there is a strong movement within many black denominations, the NAACP and the SCLC to no longer accept what is termed "status quo" thinking. The issue of the so-called "glass ceiling" keeps coming up. The bottom line from all our reports, and they have been varied and scientific, is that there is some kind of plan for a racial war in America. The phrase, "The Second

The Great Journey

Revolution," is one that is recurrent. I am further removed from all of this than you since New Jersey is more multicultural than North Carolina, and as a senator, I am not rubbing shoulders with people as much as you are. I don't know if you are acquainted with a Terrence Brown or not."

"No, I have never heard of him."

"The CIA has a whole file on him. He is an extremely capable person, graduated tops in his class from Harvard Law School, and is a former Green Beret. He even trained not too far from here at Fayetteville's Ft. Bragg. He has been a key leader not only within the NAACP but also the SCLC, and word is that he on the whole determines the direction especially of the former organization. He has a network like you and I would not believe. Though most are unaware of it, he probably would win the contest for one of the most influential people in America today, though his influence is somewhat clandestine among whites. Word is that he is tight with your friend Thomas Jackson, and I am wondering if you can get some inside information."

"Al, this sounds like the proverbial 'caught between a rock and a hard place' to me. Thomas and I are best of friends, and I would not do anything to betray his confidence. It really goes beyond just an ethical thing, if you know what I mean; it is deeper than that. I will try to find out what is going on, but I must tell you that I cannot betray confidences."

Angus found himself disturbed over this recent revelation. He and Thomas had been working hard over the last year concerning the issue of racism not just in the South, but had targeted key cities and influential people to help with the cause. He found himself, only momentarily, wondering if his lifelong friend was being up front with him. Was Thomas more of a politician than Angus's politician friend? Did Thomas indeed know something about the alarming news he had just re-

The Call

ceived? Angus knew that if what he had heard from Al was true, then the implications were portends for a racial war, not just sporadic riots. He was aware of the organizational genius especially of the NAACP and the power of the black clergy to mold and formulate an agenda for a group which numbered about forty million.

Angus had spent some time contemplating the various "isms" with which he was familiar—classism, ageism, sexism, and even denominationalism. But it seemed to him that the propensity toward racism was something which came even more naturally to most. That which is seen as different is viewed as either neutral, strange, or dangerous. He knew that several dismal chapters in American history have revolved around the issue of race and the immigration of many other nationalities to America. After all, the Irish had been the subject of intense hatred in the last century, as well as the fully Caucasian Eastern Europeans. He knew enough about Jewish history to know with certainty that their struggle was not confined just to the Holocaust, but they had been the subject of intense racism throughout the centuries. He wondered about himself; was it possible that he too harbored some form of bigotry, perhaps even unknown to himself? He prayed to God that he would not be an unworthy prophet, holding some form of imagined superiority even without his awareness.

Angus knew well the issues he had heard for years from various blacks. Many cited the long litany of injustices inflicted upon them by the white race beginning with Captain Cook's arrival in 1619 with several slaves. He had been told innumerable times, though he had not personally researched this, that close to one hundred million blacks had perished in the long journey from West Africa to the eastern seaboard of America over a period of about 250 years. Many were killed; others died of disease or storm-related incidents.

He wandered in his thinking, imagining some of the horrors of slavery on American soil until Lincoln's Emancipation

The Great Journey

Proclamation of 1863. He had read of the injustices inflicted upon black women as well; some were used as mere sexual objects by morally debauched white plantation owners. He imagined scenes at various slave markets throughout the states such as the restored one he was so accustomed to seeing in Fayetteville. He could picture the pathos of young children herded like cattle away from their parents, the estrangement of husbands and wives from one another, but perhaps, in a sense, worse than all of this was the humiliating degradation of the whole institution.

Being a preacher, he always saw the theological issues, and the fact was, he reasoned, many did not honor blacks as human beings made in God's image. In fact, for years the law claimed that a black man is only three-fifths of a person. A black woman did not count at all.

He had studied how through the latter years of the nineteenth century and well into the mid-twentieth century, blacks continued to be treated on the whole unfairly, and in many cases with great contempt. He knew all too well the phrase, "the glass ceiling," which meant that though there was no longer literal slavery in America, one's race could keep him/her subjected to a lifetime of categorized servitude. Angus was also aware of the problems among blacks themselves, which were not merely white stereotypical categorizing, such as black-on-black violence, the absent male figure within the family, the high rate of sexually transmitted diseases, and the tendency to judge the entire present Caucasian race for the past history of slavery in America. He could well understand the rage, the seething, boiling, acrimonious hatred of anything white. He found that his prayers, thoughts, and studies were often consumed with the subject. And he knew only God had the solution.

March of Death

There was not a black leader on the horizon who could rally the leadership of black America. Though Martin Luther King had left a legacy, his death in April 1968 assured what seemed to be in the minds of many a permanent vacancy in leadership. There were those of both races who still argued that King was more symbol than substance, that only in retrospect did he appear larger than life. Many whites resented Martin Luther King Day. There were also many who questioned his personal moral positions. Potential black leaders had come and gone over the years. Most were ministers who appeared to be more involved in politics and self-aggrandizement than matters pertaining to religion and the church. The majority gave up aspiring to leadership roles because of the unavoidable comparisons to Martin Luther King. Many firmly believed there would never be one who could pick up the gavel which had been wrested from the hand of the gifted thirty-nine-year-old minister when he met death in Memphis by the assassin's bullet.

Though certainly not lacking in charisma, Louis Farrakhan's style and message were seen as polarizing and generally ineffectual. The idea of a Million-Man March seemed to many to be terribly exclusive; women were not so tacitly omitted. Also, his association with Islam and his anti-Semitic stance in the minds of many excluded him from candidacy for leadership. The silver-tongued Jesse Jackson, though at times helpful, was viewed with suspicion since he was perceived by many as actually part of the white establishment. Without a doubt he was an inspiring speaker and had been in the inner circle with King, but overall he was not able to elicit the confidence of other black leaders. A leader was needed, but who?

Angus Clark and Thomas Jackson were teenagers during the period of the racial riots in Newark during the summer of 1967. They recalled vividly the images that hammered out of their televisions during that seemingly endless summer. Years before this period, they remembered the highly publicized long march to Selma, Alabama. They had grown to their adult years in separate parts of the country, attended different seminaries, were pastors of different mega churches in Charlotte, and certainly were not alike in temperament. But there was no mistaking their commitment to the cause that they believed ultimately came from God. They were not like so many who had entered the ministry from mixed motives ranging from a secure profession to perceived prestige. Rather, both had what they termed a personal "calling"; both were convinced that what they were doing was ultimately God's work and not their own.

They had first become acquaintances during their tenth year, while playing on the same Little League team. Being the same age, they found that they had several mutual interests. Thomas had been advised over the years by his mother not to hang out with any of the white boys; she told him you could not trust them, and he felt this way from personal experience as well. Still, Thomas felt that there was something about Angus which was likable. Not only was he a good shortstop,

March of Death

but he acted as if Thomas was just one of the team. Angus even found himself invited a few times to Thomas' home that was in a section of town into which he was strongly advised by family members never to venture. At first he sensed the reservation on the part of Thomas' mother, brother, and sister, but after several visits, he had lost any fear of such visits, and he always welcomed the opportunity. Angus' parents were more reserved, and while they did not discourage their friendship, they frequently suggested that he befriend those in his own neighborhood. Over the years, the two kept in contact, but by the time of their second year of college, they had not spoken for over a year. Thirty-two years later, they would find themselves on a team again, a team of only two; but the stakes were much higher this time.

Angus, a distinguished-looking man, powerfully built, slightly under six feet with thick graying hair and mustache, had a quiet commanding persona about him. His eyes were clear and blue, riveting out of a ruggedly handsome face which was beginning to show creases resulting especially from the stress of the past few months of turmoil. He was steady and sure; his voice could be thunderous, but at first impression one might consider him to be on the mild side. He spoke spontaneously, even though at times he appeared to be measuring his words. The average person would consider him a joy to speak with and would leave with the feeling that it would be a pleasure to converse with him again soon. He walked with an ever-so-slight limp, the result of a college sports injury.

Angus knew as a child that he wanted to be a minister even though he was not certain what all that involved. Being Presbyterian, some of his college buddies ribbed him for what they thought was taking the Christian faith too seriously, and those who knew something about theology, never tired of teasing him about his interest in Calvinism. As a standout on Davidson College's baseball team, he was in a sense seen as one of the boys, though perhaps more single-minded than your average college student. But those days were long past, and the years had been good to him. One would not have guessed him to be fifty.

He had an adoring wife, Sarah, and two daughters who were students at Duke University, Elizabeth and Angela. They had not been above being the typical caricature of preacher's kids, "PK's" as they were sometimes called. They were at times mischievous. Angus thought that as teenagers they would never tire of mimicking church members, especially the older ladies, or of attempting to wear various items of clothing which he and Sarah considered most inappropriate for preacher's children. One of their favorite pastimes was timing their father's sermons and reminding him of their extended length. As children, they loved to play hide-and-seek as well as other games in the church. But the two congregations he had served—one in Morristown, New Jersey, where he had served for twenty years, and his current church in Charlotte—adored them as a family.

He met Sarah during his last year in college and they married in the summer between his second and final year of seminary. She had come from a long line of preachers. Her father, Richard Holtzman, had pastored many of the leading churches in the Southern Baptist denomination. Possessing keen intelligence, warmth and beauty, she was one of those rare individuals whose magnetism was immediately apparent. More intuitive than Angus, she was able on many occasions to see the implications of decisions and give advice which even his entire board many times did not fully percieve.

Thomas was tall, six feet five inches. He had played several seasons for Dean Smith's basketball team at Chapel Hill. He was good at basketball, really good. There was no doubt either in Coach Smith's mind or his teammates that he could almost pick the basketball franchise with whom he wanted to play. Several of the winning games during his senior year at Carolina were credited to his superior ball handling skills. He was particularly strong with his famous turn around dunk, and though there were plenty of players taller than he, his opponents were sure he had special springs in his shoes. His goal had been professional basketball until he received what he termed "my calling." He had to especially endure the ridicule of his family and friends who had become convinced that he was having some kind of emotional crisis. Why would anyone give up the opportunity to play professional basketball to entertain a "calling" which certainly promised neither the financial stability nor the prestige of professional sports?

Though he was raised an Episcopalian, he decided to attend a Baptist seminary. A natural leader, he elicited the respect of his professors who predicted that he would go far in the ministry. He did have a tough time, though, with his Hebrew and Greek. But he more than made up for this lack in his preaching classes. At the conclusion of the three-year curriculum, not only had he acquired his master of divinity degree, but also had finely honed his skills which would serve him well in the ensuing years.

He vaguely remembered the hard years of the 1950s, but the decade of the 1960s was much more vivid to him since those were his teen years. Thomas wondered what it all meant. He often wondered why whites hated him. He secretly wished that his skin were lighter. As a child, he had one traumatic experience with a group of white boys who knocked him off of his bike, encircled him, pushed and flung him in the air like a sack of potatoes, and finally threw him to the ground and jumped on him in a dog pile. He could still vividly recall the

The Great Journey

feeling of suffocation; he remembered well that he thought he would die or at least lose consciousness. An older white boy who had seen the whole episode from a distance yelled at the group to let him go. Many times in the ensuring years, Thomas wondered if that person was perhaps an angel.

But what hurt more than the physical abuse were the names which were snarled at him such as "nigger," "sambo," and "chocolate boy." He vowed that he would always be vigilant around those of light complexion. Most of his experiences with whites elicited mixed feelings within himself. Sometimes he was tolerated, other times he was invisible, but primarily, he felt ignored. In his child's mind, he thought that he was the only one who was being singled out. It was not until he inquired of his friends that he discovered the treatment was not reserved for him alone, but all those who had a dark complexion had such desperate experiences. Most said that what hurt most was being treated as if you were invisible.

In July 1959, the ten-year-olds, Thomas and Angus, spent a lot of time together. Stepping into Angus's home, Thomas saw a world he had never known before. Located midway up the winding stairs on the wall was the oil portrait of a Confederate general. "Who's that?" he inquired.

"Who?"

"The picture of that man in the army."

"Oh that's my great-great-grandfather. Never knew him, but my daddy says that he loved horses. Dad even told me that one reason he became a veterinarian was because he loved horses as much as his great-granddaddy."

Thomas stared at the picture for some length of time. It seemed to him that the man in the picture looked stern and kind at the same time. He thought that the piercing blue eyes were following him.

March of Death

"Did he like colored people?" softly inquired Thomas.

"I'm sure that he did. My dad says that he was good friends with someone named Robert E. Lee; Daddy says that both of them were 'gentlemen.' They were first friends at some big school up north called West Point."

"Did he have slaves?"

"I don't know if he did or not. No one has ever said anything about that to me."

"We studied in school about that war. I think it was called the silver, ah . . . that is not right . . . the Civil War, the War between the States. My teacher told us that a lot of colored people died in that war too."

"His name was Thomas Clark. He was taken prisoner somewhere in New York, and he died there during the war. I guess that the Yankees paid him back because he was involved in a Confederate prison in Salisbury. Dad told me some stories about that place. At one time there were over ten thousand Yanks there.

"There was a prison for Yanks in Salisbury?"

"Yeah, Dad said that even David Livingstone's son was a prisoner there toward the end of the war."

"Who's David Livingstone?"

"I think he was some missionary to Africa about a hundred years ago."

"Was he colored, Angus?"

"David Livingstone? No, he was a white man. I remember reading something about him in Sunday school one time. He

The Great Journey

believed that God told him to go to Africa so the Africans could hear about Him."

"What was it they needed to hear?"

"My dad said he preached the gospel to them."

"Gospel?"

"I think that it means good news."

"Why is it good?" questioned Thomas.

"He told them about God and how much He loved them."

"I think I would have liked David Livingstone."

"My mom told me even before she was born, a lot of my people wanted to leave the South and go north. They thought that they could have a better life there. But she said that for most of them it was not any better. Many could not find jobs. She said many told her it was too cold up there."

"I sure miss my dad—he's been gone now for two years."

"What did he look like?" inquired Angus.

"Daddy was big. Did I tell you that he was a heavyweight boxer? I remember ... I think it was about three or four years ago that Daddy told me that he once fought two famous people. One was named Joe Louis and the other was Rocky something. I forget his last name. Daddy did not win either one, but he told me he boxed all rounds with them. He was always smiling. I will always remember the many times that he told me, my brother, my sister, and Mama that he loved us. I'll never understand why anyone wanted him dead. They must have been terrible people."

March of Death

Before he could say anything else, Angus's twelve-year-old sister, Amy, rushed in quickly and curtly interrupted, "Angus, I need to speak to you right now." They left Thomas alone as they hurried to another room.

"What is he doing here? Why did you invite him here? A couple of my friends saw him come over, and both of them just called about it."

"Sis, you have heard me talk about Thomas. Both Dad and Mom have met him, and they like him. He's a great basketball player."

"Angus, don't you know that we don't hang out with those people! Some of my friends said that they are dangerous, and that the best thing for anyone to do is to keep as far away as possible. That way you won't get hurt by them because I guess that they are stronger than white people. Are you sure that Mom and Dad said it is OK?"

"Yeah, he's been over here a couple of times already. I guess that you weren't here."

"But Angus, you are popular and have lots of friends—white friends. I bet none of them have darkies for friends. So why do you have to be different from everybody else?"

"Sis, I don't care to be like everyone else. I'm not into judging anyone by what he looks like, how much money his parents have, or where he lives. Thomas is my friend, and we like hanging out together. He's a real good basketball player. Dad has told me several times that he thinks Thomas is neat too."

"Does he do anything besides play basketball?"

"He has a paper route. He gets out of bed every morning while we're still sleeping and delivers hundreds of papers. Though she was somewhat scared at first, Amy discovered

The Great Journey

that Thomas was very likable. Several of her friends told her how helpful and kind he always appeared to be. After a few weeks, she always looked forward to his visits.

The corridors and several rooms of the Clark's home were lined with exquisite cherry paneling. Thomas had never seen air conditioning before, and he found that on a hot, sticky day in July when his clothes were soaked with sweat, this was the perfect place to be. The house always had a faint smell of cherry pipe tobacco—a habit that Angus's father hung onto for life. The chandeliers both in the foyer and dining room danced with radiance and gentility from the sixteen-feet high ceilings. The brightly painted and wall papered rooms seemed to smile cheerfully. The manicured bushes and lawn made the time spent during the early evenings on the porch even more inviting.

When Thomas was only seven years of age, his father died mysteriously one night after working the second shift at a cotton mill located in Kannapolis, NC. His body, which was finally found dumped in a culvert on a country road, had been riveted with at least twelve bullets according to the local coroner. Thomas's father, Henry, was a large man who had been a heavyweight, semi-professional boxer. Yet, he was called the "gentle giant" by his friends; his family just referred to him as "Daddy." The theory was that his murder had been carefully planned. There was a great deal of suspicion about the Ku Klux Klan's involvement. The Grand Dragon of the Southeastern States of the KKK had been questioned extensively, but there was no compelling evidence to link him or his chapter to the killing.

At the insistence of family and their personal lawyer, the investigation took longer than usual for such cases since the area had a long history of similar episodes. Those responsible for the undertaking appeared not to be taking the investigation too seriously. There began to be talk about a cover up.

March of Death

Thomas loved his father. He would especially miss the times they had played basketball and taken short trips together. The official report stated that there were no supects for the murder. After two years, the case was closed.

One thing his father had instilled in his precocious child at an early age was to do his very best at anything he tried. His advice reaped rich dividends in his son's life who eventually was nominated as a Morehead Scholar, the first in the history of his high school. Sometimes Thomas was the subject of not only ridicule, but also hatred by other blacks, who failed to understand his drive and the almost total lack of defensiveness in his personality. Years after his college basketball days, he still had the look of an athlete, and like his father, his physique remained stately, his shoulders square. His voice and demeanor were nothing short of commanding. His wife of twenty-five years, Sonya, and he had one child, James, who had just begun a legal practice in Raleigh. Sonya had been a varsity cheerleader at Carolina, and they were married a month after graduation.

※

Angus's family were true Southerners; he could trace his ancestry back to the early eighteenth century to a small farming community in eastern North Carolina. He recalled as a child both his maternal and paternal grandparents, who during the late 1950s lived in Fayetteville, which during those post World War II and pre-Vietnam years was a bustling city, boasting of its tobacco markets and its important military base, Ft. Bragg.

But as a child he often wondered about what really took place at the slave market that still stands in the middle of the city. He could picture the incredible pathos that occurred incessantly as families were separated, never to see one

The Great Journey

another again. In his childlike imagination, he was certain that the very streets cried out with horror of the former beating of and bartering for human flesh. But not anyone he knew, not even his family members, spoke of or imagined such things, so he kept his thoughts to himself. As a teen, he read a book called *Black Like Me* which was given to him by a friend. It described a white man disguising himself as a black man and his multiple experiences of rejection and antagonism. As Angus read the book, he realized that the work indeed described the kind of life with which he was most familiar, that is, members and friends of his own family seemed to forget their Southern affability when the subject of race relations emerged.

His father, Dr. Garfield Clark, had graduated from the University of Georgia School of Veterinary Medicine. He first practiced in Greensboro with a vet thirty years his senior. He was thankful for the experience, but decided after a couple of years that it was time to have his own practice which he bought in Fayetteville, located about a hundred miles southeast of Greensboro in the sand hills of the state. For several years, his mother Katherine, who had been a nurse at a local hospital, decided to forego those responsibilities in order to assist her husband. Though Angus's family was by no means racist, the terms "darkies" and "colored" were the standard words used to describe those who would later prefer to be called "Afro-American," and then eventually the current preference, "Afri-American." He could easily recall the segregationist mentality of those years with separate water fountains in department stores, special seating places in theaters and on buses, separate waiting rooms in doctors' offices, and of course, segregated elementary, junior high, and senior high schools. However, he always thought it was somewhat curious that his father employed black help at his clinic, and that both sets of his grandparents several times a week had colored couples help with both interior and exterior chores. His family always treated them with respect and spoke kindly

March of Death

about them; however, there was at least a silent understanding that this would be the extent of their interaction with people of color. Anything of a social nature was never even suggested. But during those years, he reasoned, "That is just the way things are."

His grandparents and parents belonged to the Highland Park Presbyterian Church in Fayetteville. Most of its members were doing well financially, living in fine houses for those years. The majority were desirous that racial issues be left as they were; better yet, it was believed that one should not bring up the subject and live as if a large percentage of the population were invisible. After all, he was informed that there were certainly more substantial issues than that of race relations. As a child, he would speak from time to time with Negroes, but except for a few of children he never really had much conversation with those whom he was taught were different and had their own special places not only to sit, go to school, and go to work, but also to live. Angus's cousin, Jimmy, who was two years older than he, told him of a time he and his brother had nothing better to do almost immediately after they got their driver's licenses, than to go to "colored town." Somehow they managed to antagonize three teens who attempted to get into their car in order to "teach them a lesson." According to Jimmy, he and his brother, David, managed to slam the door on the left arm of one of the intruders, carrying him a few feet in the attempt to get away. Since no one was seriously hurt, nothing ever came of the incident.

It was the last day in June 1965, when sixteen-year-old Angus was in the middle of town in Fayetteville. He had spent several hours looking for just the right baseball glove, but had thus far been disappointed. For the first time, he noticed that there were more crowds than usual; people of all ages and both races, black and white, were not just shopping and conversing, but were now staring up and down the

The Great Journey

streets. Then he heard several people talking excitedly about a parade which was to be held. He had not heard of any parade being scheduled for that day, and so he was both curious and excited. Notices of parades were always placed in the local paper a week before the event, so he found this talk indeed curious. In just a few minutes, the streets were lined with crowds; it seemed that the people had magically appeared, everything was happening so quickly. Because he was in the back row, he could not see what was coming one block away, but he heard people shouting, cursing. and swearing in a way he had never heard before. He heard threats of beatings and killings. The words, "poor white trash" and "nigger" seemed to echo back and forth in the crowd in snakelike rhythm. He realized for the first time the very large gathering of colored people in attendance and wondered what could possibly be in downtown Fayetteville that would draw so many from their own part of town.

He managed to squeeze to the front row, and about two hundred yards away he saw a sight he had only seen before a couple of times in history books and in the local newspaper—figures dressed in white robes, walking ten abreast, thirty rows deep, down the middle of Main Street. The words "the Klan" reverberated up and down the crowds in syncopated cadence. He looked around to his right and noticed several policemen, but it seemed to him that they were acting most casual and nonchalant about the scene. Observing their raucous laughter, he concluded that they were trading jokes. He heard several blacks whose sneering and cursing were aimed at the police, and then he was aware of the angry countenances of colored people of all ages who were stationed mainly on the opposite side of the street. Angus intently watched their faces and noticed the variety of expressions. There were those who gawked, many whose faces were twisted while they jeered, a few using hand gestures, and yes, a few who with hands folded appeared to be

March of Death

praying. Silently he wondered what was the substance of those prayers.

He had the strange sensation that time slowed down; the troop of three hundred men moved en mass to some unknown destination. It was as if history was being both relived and made. In his imagination, he could hear the sounds of the bartering for human flesh once again as it would had been over one hundred years ago in the restored city slave market. A man's value was only how large his muscles were while many white plantation owners were apparently interested in especially light-colored women. Child cries out for parents, wife shrieks for her disappearing husband, father bids farewell to son and daughter, were images which screamed through his mind.

It seemed to Angus that the Klansman in the center front row, who was also the largest, was both sneering and laughing as he swaggered past him. Most were grimacing; some had a dazed-like look in their eyes. Angus caught himself wondering what it was that they were thinking; most of all he could find no answer within himself as to why this was taking place on this day. He wondered what their backgrounds were, their families, traditions, friends, education, and jobs. He had heard his parents say many bad things about the KKK. They had even said that some of them had been involved in killing. He remembered that Thomas had one time told him that he was very afraid of them, and that he did not want to be out after dark because one of them might be waiting for him.

Then it happened—heavy gunfire! He was not sure where the shots came from, but it sounded as if the shots had been fired right behind him. Two frontline Klansmen were hit in the chest and fell to the pavement. Angus watched in stunned horror as other Klansmen were hit. He noticed that one of them was crawling toward the other side of the street, the one lined with blacks. He had an awful look of anguish stamped

The Great Journey

on his face; he held one hand over the blood-squirting, gaping wound in his chest while he managed to crawl ever so slightly with the other. Angus was sure that he heard the man cry out, "God help me!" He was sliding in his own blood. As he groveled toward the group, no one offered him any help, all stepped back; the moment seemed frozen in time. The other Klansman did not move after falling. His hood had fallen off revealing a young man with blond hair.

Later Angus learned that two Klansmen had been killed. What he had witnessed seemed to take an eternity, but the events actually occurred in about thirty seconds. Horror struck, Angus was motionless until he was aware of being thrown to the ground and trampled upon by the retreating crowd. He lay unconscious for about an hour according to a doctor who was a spectator. Fortunately, his injuries were not severe and a man who was a family friend drove Angus home.

This short episode on that hot June day would be another link in the long chain to assure race relations would never be the same in Fayetteville, or in America. Though the evidence was very sketchy, a black man, Otis Redfern, a local drunk, was charged with the murders. He was electrocuted only two months after the guilty verdict.

Beginning of a Dream

Like a resurrected Old Testament prophet, he emerged from obscurity to eventually thunder forth an electrifying, history-shaping message. His August, 28, 1964, "I Have a Dream" speech is perhaps as familiar to the world as Lincoln's November 19, 1863, Gettysburg Address. Martin Luther King, Jr.'s mystique continues to grow rather than to diminish. In 1983, many states balked at the idea of a special holiday to recognize him, but by the year 2000 every state except South Carolina acknowledges the day. Even the conservative, tradition-bound Roman Catholic Church has initiated discussions concerning his inclusion into the Church's official list of select martyrs. Few would deny his oratorical and leadership abilities. Questions concerning his personal moral ethics continue, especially among other black leaders. There would continue to be many who willingly would accuse him of womanizing and communist sympathies.

The question of who this man was continues to be posed, and the answers are varied. Many would suggest that though he possessed many gifts, as every human being does, he does not merit his present status. Another interpretation is that while his greatness is recognized, he has been deprived of the mythic status of Lincoln. Yet another interpretation borders on the common tendency when attempting to interpret any significant individual—engaging in the practice of hagiolatry, or making the person under investigation greater than the

The Great Journey

evidence merits. People from a variety of racial backgrounds probably fall into one of the three, or maybe some kind of combination of these interpretations.

Martin Luther King, Jr. was born January 15, 1929, in Atlanta. The son of a Baptist minister, he was ordained into the ministry at the young age of seventeen. After graduating from Morehouse College and Crozier Theological Seminary, he studied at Boston University receiving his Ph.D. degree in 1955. King's major emphasis concerning civil rights revolved around the Indian word *satyagraha*, or nonviolent resistance, which conclusion was the result of reading the works of Mohandas Ghandi. Married to Coretta Scott in 1953, he was the father of four children. After serving as pastor of the Dexter Avenue Baptist Church in Montgomery, Alabama, he joined his father in 1960 as copastor of the Ebenezer Baptist Church in Atlanta. By this period in his life, he had been jailed several times, had his home bombed, and had received several threats on his life. His founding of the Southern Christian Leadership Conference assured that he would be an influential leader. In 1964, he became the youngest recipient of the Nobel Peace Prize. King lamented that the Vietnam War took national attention away from the struggle for racial equality. Also, he began to feel somewhat betrayed since he initially thought that redemption would come from the North, but eventually he realized that racism permeated both the South and North.

Many believe that by the mid 1960s he was aware that he did not have much time left. Shortly before his murder, his prophetic statement, "I have been to the mountain top and seen the Promised Land," foretold his awareness. Like Moses, he would not be able to enter the Promised Land of racial equality to which he had been leading his people. He was assassinated on April 4, 1968.

Beginning of a Dream

Theories abound about just who was responsible. The King family remains convinced that his murder was not at the hands of James Earl Ray, but was the result of a larger conspiracy. Like John F. Kennedy who was assassinated four and a half years previously, the controversy of just who was involved and why continues.

Not just on Martin Luther King Day, but especially in recent years, Americans and indeed many around the world are aware of the magnitude of the influence of this man. It is not easy to peg his theology. At times he reminds one of a fundamentalist preacher with his emphasis on the Bible as the Word of God and Jesus Christ as the only Savior for humanity. Though it has historically been the liberal side of Protestantism that has esteemed him the most, in recent years those who are more conservative have begun to look seriously to his life and thought. His message was not difficult to grasp; he spoke of justice, hope, faith, love, and the expectation that one day all races would be on equal ground. Some claim that his mission has begun to be fulfilled. Others believe that racism is as blatant as ever, though perhaps it is expressed in other ways. However one interprets Martin Luther King, Jr., there is no question that his legacy is great and continues to grow.

Young Terrence Brown sat across from the internationally known leader and an auspicious group seated at the large conference table in Atlanta's Fairmont Hotel. Most of the members had the visible trappings of wealth and power with their expensive suits and coiffured hair. The inclusive conclave was comprised of several white men and women lawyers and clergymen from northern cities except for two who had practiced law in Dallas and Savannah. Martin Luther King, Jr. had convened the joint SCLC and NAACP

The Great Journey

meeting for the purpose of determining if there should be a march in Memphis. The atmosphere was tense with expectation and excitement on that chilly January 19, 1968, evening in the heart of the old South.

The minister began the meeting with prayer petitioning the Lord to watch over the country and especially their deliberations that evening. His prayer was longer than usual and was unrehearsed and so natural that it was as if he were speaking to One who was visibly present. He addressed Him in an intimate manner, and the others had the privilege to listen in on the conversation. His prayer centered on the hope that the Lord would cause peace to reign instead of hatred and strife. At the conclusion of his prayer there was an en mass "amen."

After more informal greetings and designating one to take notes of the meeting, he commenced the meeting. "Ladies and gentlemen, I warmly greet all of you and thank you for coming from various parts of the country in order to be with us tonight. I am aware that you have most busy schedules, but I believe that our time together now is very important."

The meeting continued with reviewing various civil rights setbacks and positive advances. This was the first time that there had been a joint meeting of both the SCLC and the NAACP, and initially there had been some jockeying concerning who would chair the meeting since many of the members of the NAACP believed that their agenda differed somewhat from that of the SCLC. However, two weeks before the meeting, all were in agreement that the Rev. Dr. King should convene the meeting. After four hours of lively discussion, as previewing of the coming months began, the tone of the meeting, which had been positive and lively, changed to one of an atmosphere of foreboding.

Beginning of a Dream

Voicing the concerns of the committee members, Terrence Brown stated, "Martin, I have been instructed by the executive committee to ask you not to go to back to Memphis the second time to lead the sanitation strike. You were just there last week, and we all know that the rival black power group is responsible for the death that took place. But guess what? There are many who hold you responsible since you left almost immediately after the murder. All of our careful research points to the city being a caldron of racial agitation. We just have a bad feeling about you going back a second time to the situation in Memphis; the city seems to be a hotbed of racial agitation. Several present tonight have made allusions to J.F.K. and the strong advice he received that he should not go to Dallas."

Always confident in his demeanor, King replied, "You don't know how much I appreciate your concern; ya'll continue to show how much you love me. But after much prayer, I am convinced that this is the next action which must be taken. The sanitation strike in Memphis is of utmost importance if we are to be taken seriously. Besides, the agenda has already been set, and almost every minute has been scheduled meticulously. I do not see any way possible that we can call off this strike which we all agreed on by unanimous vote just one month ago. Yes, I obviously left last week, and I now know that that was a big mistake; I must right my error."

The ensuing discussion primarily concerned security, but also if the strike was even necessary. Several cited a litany of undercover investigations which had been conducted by the CIA and FBI. One of the white lawyers, James O'Malley, had a startling revelation.

"Martin, as you know I have an inside track with the CIA and have had such for over a decade. There are an influential few who are convinced that what you are all about is dangerous for the well-being of the country. They are not necessarily

The Great Journey

racist, but they say that they are sick of the whole Martin Luther King thing and they believe that there should be an end to the movement. I have not heard any specifics since they know of my connection with you, but I know enough to realize that there could be danger from the very group who is supposed to have your well-being in mind."

It was obvious that King was startled by this revelation. "James, how could this be? The very people who are supposed to be guarding us may in fact be our enemies!"

"I am just saying, Martin, that you are going to have to watch your back if you go ahead with this Memphis plan. We can only provide so much protection for you. You actually have many enemies who will be present there including other black power groups, the KKK, some law enforcement officers, possibly the CIA and the FBI, and who knows what else waits for you there."

He was finishing his senior year of high school, and the 1968 spring break was just right around the corner. One thing about Thomas Jackson was certain—he could pick the college where he would attend on a full basketball scholarship. He had done well academically in school; many thought he was marvelously well-rounded considering all that he had been through during his eighteen short years. Though he appeared happy and outgoing, there was a terrible wound in his soul which had never healed. He still recalled the memories of his father with great affection and longing. He hid his anger well, though. Over the years, he harbored a burning rage against whites because he instinctively knew that some of them had maliciously taken the life of one whom he loved so completely. To add to the feelings of rage and betrayal, the murder, he believed, had been covered up

Beginning of a Dream

by a group of law enforcement officers who supposedly were to protect him and his family. He had managed to have a few acquaintances who were white, but even those he was able to keep emotionally at a distance—all except for one—Angus Clark. They had been close friends for the past eight years; he recalled with affection their friendship over the years spanning back to childhood when Angus would spend time with him and his family. Thomas remembered the snide remarks of his relatives and friends who questioned why he would want to not only hang out with a honkie, but actually be best friends with him. But they had been spending less time together over the last year. They had been accepted at different colleges; Thomas planned to attend Chapel Hill on a basketball scholarship while Angus would be attending Davidson College.

Thomas felt torn. On the whole, he had played it safe as he had never been involved, at least publicly, in taking sides concerning racial issues. North Carolina's largest city during the decade of the 1950s and 1960s was Charlotte, which was essentially a quiet Southern town, and there really had never been much racial polarization either in Charlotte, Raleigh, or within the state. Most blacks accepted their allocated status. He had followed, at least in the news and in conversations with friends and family members, the ministry of Martin Luther King, Jr. Thomas never could relate with Malcolm X and his Islamic religion. It was primarily his message of retaliation and the need for blacks to arm themselves and prepare for battle that repelled Thomas. How different, he thought, was the message of nonviolent resistance as preached by King. Thomas was aware that some of the members of the press as well as other hate groups were quick to assert that the so-called message of nonviolence was a smoke screen, and that King's agenda was every bit as violent as that of Malcolm X's.

The Great Journey

As Thomas continued to think about the meaning of racial issues, whether it was indeed possible for blacks and whites not just to coexist, he wondered if there was the possibility of genuine affection and not merely tolerance of one another. He recalled the friendship of the only white person with whom he had truly felt comfortable. Thomas knew that he too had taken the initiative to befriend and understand Angus, and he thought it remarkable how much of his own prejudice and misunderstanding had disappeared when he himself reached out to one of another race and background. He wondered what America would be like if all could have that same experience. Though there was much about King he questioned, such as the rumors about his personal life, Thomas felt that at least here is one who is making a major attempt to bring racial peace to America. Others like Malcolm X, the Black Panthers, various black power groups, and even the NAACP seemed to him to be destructive at worst, and polarizing at best. Also, Malcolm X's assassination in 1965 convinced Thomas that the advocating of violence only led to more violence. He saw in King one who had a true vision for America, one who did not just speak about economic parity but equality in the best sense of that term. He admired King's repeated referral to the Bible and especially the teachings of Jesus. But it was only a few months ago that Thomas had become interested in things religious.

Thomas recently had had what he believed to be a life-changing religious experience. He was raised in a family which was only nominally Christian; that is, he rarely attended church, usually only on Christmas and Easter. In retrospect, after the death of his father, he recalled that his mother seemed to be even more distant in matters relating to the church. He remembered vividly that his mother cursed God for allowing her husband to be killed; he heard her cry out late one evening shortly after the murder, "How can there be a God if my own husband was murdered!" Throughout his teen years there was no spiritual nurturing of his soul. He felt as if he were missing something, but he was not able to say exactly

Beginning of a Dream

what it was. It was as if there was a deep void within his being. One of his friends, Alonzo, told him that he was too serious and that he needed to start hanging out with them. "We'll show you a good time by drinking a few and chasing some of those wild women!" Alonzo assured him. But that really was not where his head was. He was too responsible, too level-headed for that.

In the summer between his junior and senior years in high school, he was invited to attend special evangelistic meetings at the Tryon Avenue Baptist Church in Charlotte. The only church he had ever attended was a small Episcopalian church, and then that was no more than a couple of times a year. He was accustomed to liturgy, a myriad of candles, a great deal of recitation by the congregation, and a short fifteen minute sermon which was usually read by the minister.

During spring break, a friend invited Thomas to a meeting.

"Thomas, Angie and I will pick you up tomorrow night at 6:30," promised Thomas's friend Steve. As they drove into the parking lot of the church, Thomas was curious about the many banners which had inscribed on them such phrases as, "Revival, Come Expecting a Blessing" and "Jesus Loves You."

They arrived about fifteen minutes late to a packed out church, and the usher explained to them, "The only seats we have are right up front, come and follow me."

Thomas protested, "But can't we just sit back here? I really don't want to have to parade around in front of all these people." At least, mused Thomas to himself, they were able to go when everyone was standing and singing a hymn.

The Great Journey

They were escorted to the first row, right in front of the pulpit. Someone gave him an open hymnal, and though he did not know the words, he mouthed them so he would not look so different. It seemed to him that the singing went on ad infinitum; as soon as they finished one, another one would begin. The song leader, a short rotund man with a jolly expression, encouraged the congregation of over five hundred to sing "until the rafters begin to rattle." After the fourth consecutive hymn, Thomas was certain that this was beginning to occur. Then he noticed something unusual.

"Steven and Angie, what are those two ladies doing?" inquired a startled Thomas.

He saw two middle-aged ladies slowly dancing up the isle to the front and singing out, "Thank you, Jesus," and "Lord, it's gonna be all right now." The one who was dressed in a bright yellow dress closed her eyes and stretched out her arms. It appeared to Thomas that she was going into some kind of trance. Thomas had never seen anything like this in the formal church he had occasionally attended since childhood. Then she began to go into an ecstatic dance, shaking from head to toe. Thomas wondered if she would not jerk her back out of place. The congregation began to encourage her with shouts of, "Go ahead, sister, praise the Lord," and "Jesus loves you and so do we." The affable song leader instructed the audience to cease singing, and immediately he commanded the choir of seventy-five strong voices to continue, which they did by singing more lively versions of "Swing Low, Sweet Chariot" and "When We All Get To Heaven." The members of the choir were swaying; the orchestra, the pianist, and organist gradually began to play louder. Several in the congregation could not help but join in the singing while they continued to shout words of encouragement to the lady performing the ecstatic dance. Some in the congregation stood and began to shout, "Praise the Lord." It seemed to Thomas to go on for hours, but somewhere toward the end of the episode, he found himself

Beginning of a Dream

actually caught up with what he would have first described as confusing and somewhat comical. Gradually the dancing woman, the swaying choir, orchestra, pianist, organist, and the congregation began to slowly become quiet until there was only a faint humming sound.

"What's next?" whispered Thomas anxiously.

"Oh, we are just getting warmed up. Wait until the Reverend Willie Williams comes and preaches."

Thomas really did not know what to expect. He had already seen more than he ever realized went on in any church. About the most exciting thing he had seen in the church he had attended was a Christmas play that he participated in as a child. Never did he imagine that what he had just witnessed ever occurred in a church! He looked around and saw that there were all ages present; especially there seemed to be a lot of children, teenagers, and young adults as well as those who sported gray heads. He kept thinking to himself that these people appeared to want to be here more than any other place in the world. For the first time, he thought to himself that he could now understand why so many people he knew would never want to miss church—this place was exciting!

After the choir sang "Amazing Grace," the evangelist was introduced.

The pastor of the church, Rev. Dr. Charles Price, announced, "And now the moment we have all been waiting for, the great privilege of hearing Evangelist Willie Williams declare to us the Word of God. A graduate of Southeastern Baptist Theological Seminary, he has been in the ministry for eighteen years. He served for five years as an associate evangelist with the Billy Graham Evangelistic Association. He has preached the gospel around the world literally on six of the seven continents. His most blessed crusade occurred in London where he preached for six nights in August 1987, at which crusade hundreds made decisions for Jesus Christ. He has several honorary doctorates from leading schools including one from Harvard Divinity School. It gives me great pleasure to present to you for his final message, Evangelist Willie Williams."

The evangelist had been sitting to Thomas's right several seats away; this was the first time he had seen him. Thomas, who stood six feet five inches, at first thought that the thirty-something speaker who was walking toward the pulpit looked somewhat diminutive since he was only average height. But he walked with confidence and had an air of authority about him. When he finally turned to face the audience, Thomas expired an audible, "Oh, my Lord!"

Steve in a faint whisper inquired of him, "Thomas, what is wrong?"

He stuttered, "Except for his height, that man looks so much like my father, my dad who was murdered when I was just a child. I can't believe it. Never have I seen anyone before who even resembled my father."

He was a striking-looking man with light eyes, a barrel chest, and immaculate dress. His deep, booming, resonating voice did not need to be amplified by any speaker system. He began his message slowly, almost haltingly, but after about five minutes his speaking began to crescendo. He continued, "And now let me tell you about this young man who was without hope, who did not have a father to guide him. He was considered incorrigible and was indeed a ward of the state at age fifteen. For the next three years he was shuffled from orphanage to orphanage, never believing that there was anyone who could ever love him. He engaged in every sensual delight thinking that somehow he could muffle the emotional pain that he had been experiencing for what seemed a lifetime. He became heavily involved in drugs, and this addiction led to robbery and forgery. During his eigh-

Beginning of a Dream

teenth year, he was sentenced to prison in Illinois for a term of three years. He wanted to die. It was as if life held no hope for him. But God found him by sending a prison chaplain who told him about Jesus and the fact that God loved him and would be a Father to him if he would be responsive to His love. The young man heard and accepted the gospel, and he has never been the same since. He now has purpose; he now has a true Father who never ceases to show love to him. He now delights in helping others rather than taking from them. You see, that young man is now this thirty-five year old man speaking to you this evening. . . ."

Thomas had never had feelings quite like this before. He was sure that the evangelist was speaking directly to him, and he became oblivious to the presence of the hundreds who were there with him. He believed that it was not just a coincidence that he was here this evening, and that this particular evangelist who almost could have been his father's twin was riveting a message of not only hope but also a complete paradigm shift concerning his entire life. To Thomas, it was as if his very father had somehow come back to life to give to him a message—perhaps the most important message he would ever hear in his life. He would later describe the experience by stating, "It seemed as if God Himself was speaking and telling me to come home to Him." Decades later, he would explain that that was the night that he personally experienced the love of God, and that his life was never the same again.

In the same year and month, April 3, 1968, Martin Luther King, Jr. found himself in Room 306 at the Lorraine Motel in Memphis just six days after the mayhem which caused damage to 155 stores, extensive looting, injuries to 60 people, and the death of a sixteen-year-old boy. Turning to Terrence, King lamented, "I had to return to Memphis especially since

The Great Journey

the press is saying that somehow I am responsible for last week's rioting and murder. If I didn't come back, my name would be anathamized!"

Terrence Brown, who had seen more bloodshed than anyone present since he had been involved in heavy conflict in Vietnam from 1965–1967, continued to be most reticent. Finally he yielded to King, "Martin, we will do all that we can to protect you, but you will need to be extra vigilant because we all know what is out there facing you."

At 9:00 that night King stood in front of a crowd of about 2,000 in Memphis reminding them of the need to keep pressing on. He commenced by surveying some of the great warriors from the past such as Moses who led a great mass of people out of bondage and Martin Luther who had the courage to face the greatest institution of his day in the sixteenth century. He told them that those days were exciting, but they did not compare with what God was doing in the lives of His people during these days. He concluded his directives with:

> I don't know what will happen now. We've got some difficult days ahead. But it really doesn't matter with me now. Because I've been to the mountaintop. Like anybody I would like to live a long life. Longevity has its place. But I'm not concerned with that now. I just want to do God's will. And He's allowed me to go up to the mountain. And I've looked over. I've seen the Promised Land. And I may not get there with you. But I want you to know tonight that we as a people will get to the Promised Land. So I'm happy tonight. I'm not worried about anything. I'm not fearing any man. Mine eyes have seen the glory of the coming of the Lord.

To many of those who were present that night, this speech was foreboding and lacked the positive message of his August 28, 1964, speech in Washington. Many remembered these words form his earlier speech:

Beginning of a Dream

> I have a dream this afternoon that the brotherhood of man will become a reality. With this faith, I will go out and carve a tunnel of hope from a mountain of despair.... With this faith, we will be able to achieve this new day, when all of God's children—black men and white men, Jews and Gentiles, Protestants and Catholics—will be able to join hands and sing with the Negroes in the spiritual of old, "Free at last! Free at last! Thank God almighty, we are free at last."

His rousing Memphis speech had been encouraged by a continuous round of "yes Doctor," "go ahead," "that's right," and "yes sir." Many who heard him that night commented that it appeared that he had some kind of premonition of his own death, while others believed that the message was an affirmation of life. Young Thomas Jackson stood in that crowd that night. He was in many ways the same person, but he now had a whole new dimension to him that was even more important than what he was most noted for—sports. Gradually over the months of his spiritual awakening, he had come to the realization that God had something very specific for him to do other than play basketball. He believed that one day he would be doing the Lord's work in a special way, but he just was not sure of what all that entailed. He was not thinking of going to seminary or becoming a pastor, only that he believed that he must continue to be aware of God's leading in his life.

King's brother arrived from Louisville, and the two conversed until about 4:00 a.m. on April 4; after sleeping for about five hours, Martin was roused from a sound sleep by Ralph Abernathy with the encouragement that the day promised to be a memorable one.

In the early afternoon, several radical black liberation group members managed to convene a meeting with King and their spokesman urged him, "Isn't it time that you give up on this nonviolence agenda? How far can you go with this line of thinking? Don't you know that the only thing that the white man understands is violence. With Malcolm X, we agree that we must take up arms. That's the only way we are going to be free. We think that you are letting Rosa Parks down; just think of what she had to go through. Think of all of our brothers and sisters who have been hanged, gunned down, thrown in prison, sent to death row for no good reason, and all you can talk about is nonviolence! We were slaves of the white man for almost 250 years, and though we supposedly have been free for a little over a hundred years, we are still slaves to whitey. He dictates where we work, live, hang out, and especially the size of our bank accounts. Martin, we are sick and tired of it! We know that you are a preacher and all that, but the Bible does give a whole lot of illustrations of taking care of the enemy, especially in the Old Testament. Remember, all those Egyptians who were chasing after God's people were mysteriously drowned in the Red Sea. King David surely had no problem in killing those whom he thought were the enemy. It is time now for you to decide that you are going to quit pussy-footing around and get down to action! If you make that decision right now, we will have an army here in no time to help you. All of the law enforcement in Memphis won't be able to stop us. If you continue with the way you are going, there won't be any real change in your lifetime, if ever. The spirits of all those who have been slain over the centuries will cry out to you, 'Why did you not avenge our deaths?'"

As usual, King listened with rapt attention, but continued the conversation with even more firmness, "Violence breeds violence. My understanding of the Bible is that Jesus and the New Testament advocate forgiveness and admonition to come together in a reasonable way. In fact, in Matthew 5 Jesus said something about a person being blessed if he were being persecuted. And I doubt if the spirits of the departed are going to want, even if they could, to spend too much time on me."

There ensued a heated debate on the two sides of the issue. Finally when the leader of the liberation group saw that he

Beginning of a Dream

was not going to be able to budge King, he cursed and stormed out of the motel room with his comrades.

Welcoming a respite from the already challenging day, King sat in a chair, closing his eyes and desiring simply to rest, but not for long. Terrence Brown rushed in blurting out, "Doc, I know that you are resting, but I want you to meet one who I believe would make a fine addition to our inner circle. His name is Thomas Jackson. He's young, but believe me, he has all the potential for the kind of leadership that we have been looking for recently. Jesse Jackson has met him, and his opinion is the same as mine. We both decided that he should come to meet you. He has leadership skills that we both believe could be very useful.

The two engaged in conversation for about thirty minutes. "Tell me, Thomas, what are your plans for the future?"

"Well, they tell me I can shoot ball. I have a scholarship to Carolina."

"What about after graduation?"

"Dr. King, I guess I will continue, or at least I hope to play pro ball."

"That will be at the most sixteen or seventeen years. Then what will you do with the rest of your life?"

"I have to admit that I have never thought about it. Not too long ago I had a life-changing experience. I found the Lord."

"Thomas, He will tell you what to do. Just listen to Him and you will never go wrong."

"Dr. King, I find the Bible and prayer helpful."

"Of course. But just remember, that the Lord does not promise any of us an easy life. I have been to the mountaintop, but

The Great Journey

I assure you there have been valley experiences as well. It is amazing to me that outsiders say that I live a movie-star type life. They have no idea of the pressures I constantly face. The Lord continues to see me through them."

He and Dr. King continued to talk about possible plans for the future, and how the Lord had led in King's life, and how He would do the same for Thomas.

After extended conversation, he politely dismissed Thomas. Martin turned to Terrence and congratulated him on locating one who would especially appeal to young future leadership. "I am particularly impressed with his love for matters relating to the Church," replied King to Brown's question of why he was impressed with him. "He appears to be a person of not just physical stature but mental and spiritual as well. I realize that he will be starting college soon and that his schedule will not permit him to attend many of our meetings, but we will fit him in wherever feasible and helpful for the cause."

After resting again for an hour, King commenced to get ready for the evening's activities. He and his staff had been invited to a Rev. Samuel Kyle's home for dinner. But Martin just did not feel right, and he was not sure if the feeling was caused by undo worry or if he was catching a bug. He had recently been receiving more hate mail than usual. He had always been able to act as if such letters did not bother him, but there was no mistake that the volume of such recent mail as well as what he considered the recent slanting of the press, had left him emotionally weakened. He reflected on his life. As a child he remembered his father, who was also a minister, told him that life can become difficult, but that it was during the hard times that God's grace was all the more certain. He was able to recall vividly all the details of his marches, particularly the one to Selma. The memories of his imprisonment in Birmingham were especially intense; it was as if he could close his eyes and in an instant he was there again, in places of loneliness and

Beginning of a Dream

despair, where one did not ultimately know if he would see the light of hope again, where one was totally at the mercy of a system which seemed especially keen on favoring Caucasians more so than blacks.

But he was thankful, for he realized that in his short thirty-nine years he had accomplished a great deal. Yes, God had been good to him. He not only had an earned doctoral degree from a prestigious school, but he had been the youngest recipient of the Nobel Peace Prize. He had pastored two churches, one by himself and the other with his father with whom he felt so close. He was thankful to God for his family, Coretta, and their four children. He was ever aware of his frailties, that like every human being, he in a sense had feet of clay, and he was mindful that he would answer to God for those shortcomings. He wondered why God had chosen him to carry out such a seemingly impossible task; surely there were many others who were better qualified. But over the years, he had drawn strength from the Lord's promise to the Apostle Paul when he pledged to him, "My grace is sufficient for you."

Martin put on one of his favorite suits along with a newly-acquired tie. Though he was feeling somewhat reticent about being in Memphis, he was glad that he was surrounded with so many for whom he deeply cared. He thought about Coretta and the children; he was already looking forward to the next time that they would be together again as a family. Of all his relationships, he considered his family the most precious; he cherished all five of them.

Finally dressed for the evening, he decided that he would step out of his spacious motel room to the balcony. He saw Jesse waving to him and yelled out that he wanted him to go to dinner with them. Standing on the balcony with him were Terrence Brown and Martin's new friend Thomas Jackson. Both had just returned. It was a chilly late afternoon. Both were looking directly at Martin Luther King, Jr. when they saw a sight which seemed surreal—it was as if the right side of Martin's face exploded, sending bits of flesh, bone and streams of blood spewing in a geyser-like torrent. Almost simultaneously with the ghastly sight, they heard the sound of a high powered rifle. Looking forty yards across the space to a window of an adjoining building, Thomas saw the face of a thirty-something Caucasian glaring at him with a devilish smirk. Then he vanished. But it was a face that over three decades of time could not erase from his memory.

The ensuing months passed slowly for Thomas as the haunting reminder of what had happened, and what he had witnessed repeatedly played itself out in his thoughts, conversations, and even his dreams. He wondered what it all meant. Here he claimed that he had found God in a meaningful and intimate way, but yet God had allowed this abhorrent episode to occur which impacted both the black and white races since many Caucasians, especially in the last year of King's life, had melded themselves into the movement which King led. With trepidation, he wondered what would be the final outcome of what he had witnessed on that cold day in Memphis on April 4, 1968.

4

Connection

Thomas was in a pensive mood. He had been in ministry for twenty-five years, and recently sometimes he had begun wondering about the direction of his life. Oh yes, he was now the senior pastor of one of the largest black churches in America. He was revered not only by his large congregation at Ebenezer Baptist Church in Charlotte, but also by his vast television audience. Though he still anticipated years of ministry, he felt somewhat empty. He finally figured out what the problem was—he was lacking a true friend in his life. It seemed that people held him at arm's length since he was a man of the cloth. He had had innumerable acquaintances, and these people seemed to genuinely admire him, but they were not what he would consider as solid friends. He reflected back on his childhood and teenage years and realized that he had had no close friends except for one white person named Angus Clark. As a child, he recalled how he enjoyed this friendship, even more so than with the black children and teens. Thomas knew that he had a competitive streak in him that few, especially of his own race, could appreciate. As he took a few moments to muse, he realized that he was committing a sin of middle age—reflecting on the past. When he thought about the intervening years since he had seen Angus, he was amazed how quickly time had gone.

The Great Journey

Thomas knew about Angus's ministry in Charlotte, and even though they both had begun their tenure as senior pastors at about the same time, they had not contacted one another until that day when Thomas picked up the phone and heard a most familiar voice.

"Thomas, it has been way too long, my friend!"

"This is a voice which cannot be erased even though it has been close to three decades since I have heard it."

With apparent excitement Angus explained, "I knew that you began your ministry at Ebenezer about six months after I began at New Covenant. Several times I started to call, but it seemed that something always came up."

"Same here, good buddy."

They spent over an hour conversing. Angus then asked the question that continued to mystify him, "How is it, Thomas, that you are in the ministry? When you went off to play for Dean Smith, your goal was only basketball. I really do not even recall your talking about the church. I believe I remember you did go to some church at Christmas time. In fact, as I recall, you thought I was a little strange for spending so much time at my church. Then, when I mentioned to you toward the end of our high school years that I wanted to go to seminary after college, I believe you thought I was stepping off the deep end."

"I did well at Carolina, and then played for New Jersey for three seasons, and though I had about everything anyone could want, I knew that there were more important matters to which I must give my fullest attention."

The two met the following day for several hours. Thomas related to Angus the religious experience which he had had back in 1967, something which he had never told Angus. "In

Connection

that year, Angus, I found what you had been attempting to tell me about for so long. I did not quite understand you. As you know, I really did not grow up in a family that was familiar with the church, and so when you talked to me of your faith, it seemed strange to me. But I thought that was just the way you were, and that all people have some peculiar things about them. In the condition I was, I had no awareness of how important one's personal faith is. Almost immediately after my conversion, I began to think differently. People commented that I seemed different—and, no, they did not mean peculiar! They kept saying such things as I seemed more relaxed, joyful, and compassionate. It was as if God had given to me a new soul and eyes with which to see, feel, and experience life. Life literally took on a new meaning for me. Before, all I could do was focus on myself and my problems, but almost immediately I started to be concerned about others' needs. I remembered that you had told me that you felt called to be a pastor. I never mentioned this to you then, but I thought that was most strange. Here you had this tremendous athleticism in baseball. Why would you ever want to waste your life being a preacher? But after playing several seasons in pro basketball, I still felt empty. I began to read the Bible more than I ever had, and I began to speak in churches and other places. I cannot describe the fulfillment which I began to experience. It was like nothing I ever dreamed possible. Eventually, I came to see that I was being called to the ministry. I enrolled in seminary, and ever since graduation in 1975, I have been serving as a pastor."

"Thomas, it is hard to believe that we are both pastors of two nationally-known churches. We never would have believed it as teens."

"Angus, I believe that God used you in my life as no one else could possibly have. You were so kind; you really did not have to work at it. That was just you. Your whole family was so good to me. I never did tell your father, but in many ways he became like a father to me after Daddy was murdered. That summer he allowed me to work around his veterinary clinic with you are some of the best memories of my teenage years. I often felt so lonely because other blacks acted as if they were my friends, but they really were not. I was always given a hard time because I hung around you. I had lots of acquaintances, but as far as someone I really trusted, it was only you."

Both were filled with joy because of the realization that their friendship had been renewed.

Terrence Brown had done well for himself over the span of three decades. In fact, there was a good deal of speculation that he would run for the presidency of the United States in 2004. As the president of the newly formed Coalition of Black People, he wielded great power concerning the direction of race relations in America. He was articulate, and many Americans had a keen interest in his political views, but some considered his views radical and even dangerous. Terrence Brown had been considered the likely candidate for the presidency of the NAACP, but he, along with the backing of close to 20,000, decided in 1991 to form the CBP, an organization that advocated the use of force for the gaining of political power. The Coalition of Black People had in the last four years experienced phenomenal growth, and many believed that it was only a matter of a short period of time when the new movement would outstrip the authority of the NAACP.

Terrence continued to be a regular on Larry King and recently had been interviewed on various prime-time shows. Because of his Harvard education, his skills in debate and oratory, his analytical mind, and perhaps foremost, his great courage, he had a large following. He and Thomas had kept in contact

Connection

intermittently over the years. More than any other factor, their relationship was probably based upon their mutual experience with Martin Luther King, Jr. on April 4, 1968. There was no spiritual kinship between the two since Brown considered himself only nominally Christian; that is, the term for him was almost synonymous with politics. He would never converse about the possibility of entering into a relationship with Jesus or God.

In recent months, there had been more racial agitation than usual in America's metropolitan areas. Many were continuing to complain that racism was actually worse than it was in the 1950s and 1960s. When some whites would argue that there were many blacks who had risen to the highest position possible in various fields, the usual reply was that such individuals were either "Uncle Toms" or "Oreos." Many influential blacks, especially Terrence Brown, continued to speak of the "glass ceiling," or that they felt that when blacks attempted to progress in their professions, there were white forces to halt their progress. The white power structure was usually implicated as the source of the problem. Many argued that during the 1960s the lines were drawn clearly; it was obvious who the enemy was. But now racism was seen as invisible and coming in a myriad of forms.

Brown had his enemies among his own people. There were those who said that he was the ultimate name dropper because he used the assassination of King to further his own political ambitions. Riding on the coattails of the fallen leader's reputation, he himself gained notoriety, so his detractors asserted. Some claimed that he was simply glibness without substance. For those who knew of his Green Beret days, the accusation was that he thrived on the truly dangerous. Brown had a curious personality. He could be both charming and distant simultaneously. He never married, but was rarely seen without a beautiful woman at his side.

The Great Journey

As two nationally known black leaders, Terrence and Thomas periodically had conversations concerning America's future from a minority's viewpoint. Terrence challenged, "Thomas, times have changed, and it is time that you get with it. During King's time, the nonviolence approach was fine, but no longer. The Black Liberation Army has over the recent years, convinced me that we must be more aligned with Malcolm X's agenda than with King's. If we don't start pushing for revolution, all that we worked for over the decades will be destroyed. All that we will have to show for our collective effort are a few Uncle Toms who have been hand-picked and groomed in order to assure that things continue in a politically correct way. Jesse Jackson did not have a chance to be president in 1984, and he would have even less a chance if he were running today. No, Thomas, the strictures of the white man's America are set in granite, never to be budged unless we decide to explode the edifice."

"Don't you see, Terrence, that the main problem is not a political one but a spiritual one."

"What on earth do you mean by spiritual? I know of a fortune teller down the road, and I bet she could tell us a great deal about spirits! Come on, Thomas, I know that you are a preacher and all that, but surely you have enough good sense to see that all the praying in the world will never help with the situation that our people are now facing. King was a preacher, but he surely was not afraid to lead marches and do all that he could to try to stop the evils of the white man and our society, though he too perhaps talked too much about Jesus. I remember that he preached one sermon on something called the Good Samaritan. I never did quite understand that one. Maybe King's Achilles' heel was that he spoke too much about Jesus and used him as a role model more so than someone like Marx or Stalin. I have had more experience than you, Thomas, with the ways of the world, and believe me this soft touch, wimpy approach just will not stand up to the test of time and reality. I

Connection

have been in the thick of war, and guess what? When your life is on the line, you are not going to do very well by telling the person who is trying to kill you, 'Hey it's OK, I'll forgive you, let's be friends.'"

Angered by what he saw as Terrence's lack of awareness of not only King but especially the whole Christian message, Thomas countered, "Jesus Christ, the most revolutionary figure in all of history, did not advocate violence. He easily could have vindicated himself. Believing that he is both God and human, I realize that he had all the power of the universe within His grasp. The Bible even says that He could have called angels to come to help Him. His message was about the kingdom of God; He personified truth and character. You talk about inclusivity, never has there been one as inclusive as Jesus with His claim that the gospel is for all nations. He often spoke about even loving our enemies...."

"Get with it man! I am tired of hearing about Jesus. Give me an example of a real leader, one who advocated overthrowing existing evil social structures by power. Your Jesus seems to lack in many ways. I really cannot understand why so many speak of Him as being so powerful. Supposedly, all of these views about Jesus are taken from the Bible, but most educated people today know that the Bible is full of contradictions and that it is of a human and not a divine origin. The writers of the Bible were no more inspired than say a Kafka, Twain, Shakespeare, or Hemmingway. When I was at Harvard, I would venture every now and then over to the divinity school, and I remember sitting in one professor's class. He said that the Bible is only of human origin. I don't mean to be rude; I know that you take the ministry seriously, but you might even have a more meaningful ministry if you preached from some famous writers' works, rather than only the Bible which I always found boring. Jesus did not even have the power to deliver himself from the Romans. As far as all that resurrection stuff, I have heard and read many who say it is nothing but a myth.

I hear Christians talk about a Second Coming as if when that event occurs, then all the injustices which we have endured will finally be made right. This idea again seems to me to be nothing but another myth which Christians have clung onto in order that they can use this so-called belief to make life easier. I believe the usual phrase is, 'The opiate of the masses.' I mean, for example, look at especially our people. Religion became the only way for blacks to stand the burden of slavery. They would compose those spirituals, which probably had more to do with coded language than anything else, to help them get through the day, and then what became a lifetime of torture. Had it not been for slavery, our people would not be nearly as interested in religion and Jesus as they are today. One of the ironies is that Christianity is more of a white man's religion than a black's. During the days of slavery, the white plantation owners gave them Jesus with the hopes that this religion would make the slaves even more obedient and docile. Another thing I can't quite understand is how you would go to a seminary for three years after college. I can understand why a doctor has to go four years and a lawyer three years, but why would one possibly need to attend a seminary that long if at all."

Thomas finally replied, "I can see that you have come to your conclusions with great passion, and at least you are more aware of some of the issues than even most Christians are. I respect you and will defend your right to believe as you do. We all have that freedom in America, at least at the present we do."

" That's one thing that I like about you, Thomas. You are willing to listen, and at least outwardly you are not going to condemn me. You probably are thinking that God will do that!"

Connection

"But I believe, Terrence, that any thinking person would agree that reason can take us only so far. There comes a point, and even science agrees with this, that faith is all that one can depend upon."

The Ku Klux Klan met in Atlanta for their annual national meeting. All twelve Grand Dragons comprised the Executive Council which continued in back to back meetings for four of the five days of the convention. This year's conference, which ran from July 15–19, 2000, proved to be one in which a continuous round of controversial issues surfaced. Between 3,500–4,000 members registered, but it was estimated that perhaps a thousand more were present.

The Chairman of the Board of Directors of the KKK, Ray Rubens, recently had been elected Grand Wizard, the highest position within the organization. He commenced the meeting by introducing three newly elected Grand Dragons to the others, each who had been in office for over a decade. Historically, there was one Grand Dragon for each southern state, but there were now several states outside of the South which were represented. This year's meeting was filled with great excitement and anticipation since there was an important agenda for the Board to consider.

The meetings had been long and intense, and by the beginning of the third day Tommy Johns, now Grand Dragon of North Carolina, suggested, "Let's get on with the real issues that we need to deal with. Grand Wizard Rubens, could you please tell the rest of the Board what that major issue is?"

"Well, I had been planning to bring up the topic later on today, but I believe that our agenda will make it appropriate at this point. As ya'll know, the KKK has been losing its vitality

The Great Journey

over the past decade. Actually, I think that one reason for the loss began when we started to slack up on our terrorizing of Roman Catholics. We had a good solution for all those Eastern Europeans immigrating with their weird religion. We're certainly nothing like we were back in the 1930s and 1940s. There are many reasons for this, and one important one is because of the rise of other groups that are very much like us. What I believe is necessary at this point is to form a new KKK which will be called the "United Invisible Empire." Again, I believe it is necessary to strengthen ourselves; you know the phrase 'there is strength in numbers.' Why have I chosen this name? As you know, in the nineteenth century we were known as the "Invisible Empire"; those truly were our glory days. We will once again regain that lost glory. I have spoken with the governing bodies of the Neo-Nazis, the National Association of the Advancement of White People, and a very interesting white supremacist group in the states of Nevada, Wyoming, Montana, South Dakota, Colorado, and California called The Aryan Liberation Front. This group is really exciting because it is made up of primarily women; their leader is Sylvia Helowstein. All three of these groups are willing to join ranks with us. They stand for the same things that we do—hatred of the government, Jews, Catholics, Asians, Hispanics, and of course our number one enemy—blacks. They all know of the supreme importance of maintaining the racial purity of the white race. The NAAWP at first did not want to lose its name, but after they were able to see how much they would gain, they were glad to do so.

I think that the new name of United Invisible Empire says it all. For one thing we have history on our side, going back at least one hundred and forty years. There will be two representatives form each of the three new groups, making a total of eighteen on the Board of Directors of the UIE. Without a doubt, this new movement will be an invincible force. This should bring the official membership of the new group close to 20,000. Of course, unofficially there may be three or four

Connection

times that number. What I fully anticipate is that our group will experience phenomenal growth. Why? For the simple reason that a new supremacist group is spawning almost every week somewhere in America. Through our intelligence agencies, we will be able to locate these small groups and convince them of the need to join us. When they see the benefits, there will be no problem in recruitment. By the way, the leadership of each of the three new groups has consented that I will be the head of the new organization and that I can keep my title as the Grand Wizard. I propose that we move ahead quickly with this new arrangement."

Three of the Grand Dragons had various questions concerning this new arrangement. The Grand Dragon of South Carolina, Bill Alexander, protested, "It seems to me that you did all of the arranging to benefit yourself more so than the others. There was nothing really very democratic in how this new UIE has been formed."

"Let me remind you, Mr. Alexander, I elevated you to this position in good faith that you would be a team player. No, on this issue I am making an administrative decision, and this is what I strongly advise all of you to do. I need your fullest cooperation in order to lead this God-ordained movement to new heights. Of course, Mr. Alexander, if you are not happy with what is being decided, we will gladly accept your resignation now."

The vote was taken and it was unanimous that Ray Rubens assume the new position in the UIE. The following two days were spent on a variety of issues, all the way from the raising of finances in order to support the new movement to plans for purifying the racial makeup of America. The latter issue was of no small controversy.

Rubens pontificated, "We, the true Americans and members of the superior race, are being besieged by a variety of de-

The Great Journey

generate and dangerous hoards. I don't think there is much that we can do about all these new religions which are coming from the East, and overall they probably will not pose much of a problem to us during our lifetime or even in the next one hundred years. No, we need to reactivate our fight against the Roman Catholic Church. Just think, because of this twisted religion, which is basically a one man show with the Pope, it was possible to have a Catholic in 1960 elevated to the highest position in the country. We must do all that we can to be certain that there is not a repeat of John F. Kennedy ever again.

We still have a problem with the Jews. We can be thankful for Adolph Hitler and his part in the Holocaust; at least he got rid of several million of them. I think the best we can do now is to keep continual agitation going on between them and the Islamic religion. I believe that our best comrades for this front will be the newly inducted Neo-Nazis. Hitler's final solution was not fully successful. But at least we are able to glean valuable principles from his writings and the wonderful example that he has given to us. I believe that there will continue to be great growth in numbers from those who hold to Neo-Nazism. The problem of the Jews should be eliminated in a couple of decades or so.

The real problem in America is, as we all know, the black race. When our country allowed them the same rights as whites in the 1950s and 1960s, the ultimate treason was committed. Yes, we have been and continue to be betrayed by an America which is less than a shadow of its former glory. Our forefathers must be turning somersaults in their graves because of all of this political correctness junk. It all started with Harriet Beecher Stowe and her work *Uncle Tom's Cabin*. The KKK was around then. Surely if our forefathers had been more vigilant, they could have stopped the publication of that dreaded book which was one of the main reasons for Lincoln's greatest mistake—the Emancipation Proclamation. I believe that the Aryan Liberation Front, a very power-

Connection

ful white women's supremacist group, which has now been assimilated in the United Invisible Empire, will be of utmost value in our newly upgraded war against blacks in America. Yes, the women are doing a great job.

The most recent intelligence informs us of the continued evil activity of one Terrence Brown. He is even more dangerous to the safety and continued superiority of the white race than was Martin Luther King, Jr. Yes, we should have finished him off long ago. We now know of the establishment of a new danger to all of us called the Coalition of Black People, which advocates extreme violence against whites. Reliable reports are that this movement is growing more quickly than the NAACP. This is one movement that we must continually monitor. Brown must be considered extremely dangerous. He is the president of this movement that goes by the CBP. Brown apparently is a better thinker than most blacks. With his leadership of this new movement, we will be going back to Malcolm X's days, but this time we are involved with a much larger movement; there will be perhaps hundreds of thousands of loose canons out there aimed at us. Brown must be stopped! He has also supposedly enlisted the help of several influential clergy, one of whom is the Reverend Thomas Jackson, who is the pastor of some large Baptist church in Charlotte.

It has always struck me as strange how blacks try to make us whites think that somehow God is on their side. Besides George Foreman, I have never really known any preacher who was very athletic. I remember I got into a tussle with some preacher not too long ago, and I asked him, 'What are you going to do about it, hit me over the head with your Bible?' He mumbled something about not giving pearls to swine. I don't know who I hate more, the CIA or the clergy."

The Great Journey

It had been one month since Angus and Thomas finally contacted each other again after their first connection in many years. Though both had children who were no longer living at home; nevertheless, they were very much entangled with the busyness of ministry. Not only were there the usual sermons to prepare, staff and board meetings, minor controversies within the congregations, emergency visitations, funerals, weddings, and writing, but increasingly both pastors were having to deal with the national attention which was progressively being focused on both churches.

Their churches had obvious differences other than the racial makeup, in spite of the fact that both had some racial mixture. Though not charismatic or Pentecostal, Ebenezer Baptist Church's services were lively, sometimes really so. The 14,000-member congregation was affiliated with a major Baptist denomination. It was fairly young, having been initiated by a small group in 1975. The trademarks of the church were Bible preaching, middle of the road political action groups, and great choirs and orchestras. Thomas was in an enviable position since he was the church's first and only pastor, and because of this, he wielded great authority. He never did so censoriously or in a dictatorial manner, but he usually led gently and with compassion. Of course, his 6' 5" frame gave him a commanding demeanor, but it was secondary to his leadership skills. The church had seen its share of controversies and minor splits over the time he had been the shepherd, but somehow he was always able not only to hold the church together, but also to affect great growth.

One big controversy ten years ago was over the issue of white leadership at Ebenezer. Apparently most believed that it was fine if whites wanted to attend, but when there was an attempt primarily on Thomas's part to vote for four white men and women to serve in leadership roles, many of the members became irate saying such things as "The last thing we ever want again is to have some white person directing our spiritual

Connection

lives! We endured that during slavery, and we will never again have such." The controversy continued for about a year, and the outcome was that about five hundred left to form another church. All four whites were voted into leadership positions at Ebenezer, but he was not naïve enough to think that all were now happy with the situation.

Thomas believed that his ministry should be one that was heavily involved with politics, and so it was not uncommon for him to have leading black or white state and national senators occasionally bring a message from the pulpit. Though he did not believe in the message of radical black power groups, he was concerned with the issue of true equality of all races. There was much about the legacy of Martin Luther King, Jr. he did not appreciate, but Thomas did admire the nonviolent method he took against racial injustice. He was aware of the frailties of human nature and the dangerous position one is in if he or she is elevated to a mythical status of one like King. Thomas always prayed that God would grant him wisdom and grace.

※

The Session of New Covenant Presbyterian Church had extended a call to Angus Clark as their pastor in 1991, and the 12,000-member denominational congregation had doubled in the past five years under his leadership. Though raised in the South, he had spent most of his ministerial career serving in the North at Morristown, New Jersey. He had a presence about him that inspired instant respect. Intelligent, appropriately able to use humor, empathizing easily with people from all walks of life, commanding, and never at a loss for words were customary ways of describing him. His pastorate in New Jersey had been so successful that both *Newsweek* and *Time* had devoted extensive feature articles concerning the ministry. Both the remarkable growth and

The Great Journey

the involvement of significant political figures such as the Republican governor of New Jersey were highlighted. But after a ministry of twelve years, he conceded that the Lord had other plans, and Angus accepted the unanimous call to begin in Charlotte June 1991.

The ministry of the fifty-year-old church had historically not been involved with political issues, except perhaps as an aside. Angus, on the whole, had continued in that tradition. His involvement with racial issues, however, did raise the eyebrows of many, and he began to receive escalating criticism. The memory of the boardroom fracas of two years ago did, however, leave somewhat of an emotional wound. Mr. Cornelius and some of his cronies eventually left New Covenant, taking about a hundred others with them. But since this episode had been somewhat private, the long-term implications were not as devastating as Angus had initially expected. He was becoming in a sense America's pastor, as millions tuned in to the nationally televised program. Ever the innovator, he and the other leaders of New Covenant were exploring the possibility of international coverage. Angus continued to speak several times a year in other countries; he was especially popular in Great Britain and Germany.

Angus and Thomas had been getting together at least twice a week either for a game of racketball or golf for the past month. They enjoyed each other's company, but Angus had not been aware of some of Thomas's interests and activities.

"Thomas, not too long ago Congressman Al Bartelli, whom I know well from my New Jersey days, called me. He was very active in the church I served in Morristown, and we got to know each other quite well. This is kind of touchy, Thomas, but I feel I need to ask you about it."

"I can't imagine what you are about to ask."

Connection

"Al has connections with the CIA, and Thomas—well, he knows that we are best of friends—he claims that you have ties with a Terrence Brown who is supposedly considered to be very radical and dangerous. Who is he?"

After Thomas gave Angus a long history of Terrence, Angus recollected that he did indeed know Terrence; at least he remembered him from what seemed to be a lifetime ago. As a child Angus went with his father for veterinary work at Terrence's home. Angus was one who was always careful to say, "Never underestimate the potential which one solitary individual possesses." Nevertheless, he was amazed what the child with whom he used to ride mules had become.

Thomas continued, "Angus, even though there was a hiatus of about twenty-seven years, I feel that we know just about everything about one another, or at least it seems that we do."

"I imagine that there are a few things we don't know now that would take a couple of years to divulge."

"I never told you about this; it happened our last year in high school. Remember things were pretty intense about that time, at least they were for me, with basketball season coming to a close, preparing for graduation, and making plans to attend Carolina. I had known Terrence Brown from a distance, you might say. He apparently was impressed with my basketball ability, and after some games, he would make it a point to talk with me. In my senior year, I think it was January or February 1968, he invited me to join him at a King event. I really was not all that interested in going. Had he asked me in my junior year in high school, I doubt if I would have gone. But remember I had had a conversion experience, and though I really did not understand King, I knew he was a preacher, and I guess that was my main attraction to him. You know, the only preachers I had ever known seemed kind of boring. Oh sure, some of them could hoop and holler some, but basically I saw them as people not all that talented who needed a job and were good at holding old ladies' hands. I remember thinking that most preachers seemed to be but a poor rendition of the Old Testament prophets and especially the New Testament apostles who were not afraid to tell kings and emperors that they had better get right with God. Well, I saw Martin Luther King, Jr. like those prophets and apostles; he seemed fearless to me, and of course, I knew of his large following. He seemed so sincere to me. Here was one who wasn't content to hide behind the pulpit, retreat to the parsonage, and then come out again the following Sunday. I guess that is how I used to view preachers."

"I remember Malcolm X appeared to lack compassion, at least this was my perception, and he seemed so defensive. He wanted to make the whole white race out to be demonic. To be frank, that is what bothers me about Terrence Brown today. I don't think he was like that years ago, but now he has this radical agenda which includes the view that the white race is in league with the devil. You have said this to me on several occasions, Angus, 'I am sorry for what my ancestors did, but how am I personally responsible for their sins?' At first I have to admit that explanation irritated me; it seemed to me as if you were justifying yourself at best or being smug at worst. But after considerable thought, I agree with you.

Maybe you remember that King went to Memphis first in late March of that year, and because of a near disaster, he left town very quickly only to return about a week later, the first week of April. Well, Brown invited me to join him in Memphis. It was spring break, and I thought it would be interesting if nothing else. Little did I know what waited me in Memphis!"

"I can't believe you never told me what I think you are about to tell me."

Connection

"I was there, Angus; I was with King when it happened. Terrence had taken me to the motel room where he was staying with Ralph Abernathy and others. Terrence introduced me to Martin Luther King, Jr. We spoke for about a half hour or so, and he told me that based mainly on Terrence's recommendation and his own assessment, he wanted me to be part of his inner circle. I never was so excited in all my life, Angus! Here I was not only talking to one of the most powerful men in America if not the world, but he told Terrence that he wanted me to be part of his organization. I was not that excited when I was accepted to play pro basketball with New Jersey. But then, Angus, what I saw not too much later is something that still haunts me. Terrence and I were outside on a balcony. King came out and yelled out to Jesse Jackson. He turned and looked at us, and then it happened....hearing a loud gunshot, it was as if King's face exploded. I happened to look in the direction of the sound of the shot, which really was not too far away, and I saw the face of a white man who was maybe in his early twenties. That face, it used to haunt me in my dreams... I'll never forget it."

"Thomas, I can't believe that you have been carrying this load around for this long! You are lucky to be alive. When I think of you and what you told me, I am reminded of Jesus' words, 'Physician, heal thyself.' Here you are a most successful minister; you know about counseling, the relationship of mind and body, and yet you have apparently not shared this information with anyone before."

"Not true, my wife knows all about it, along with you and Terrence. But you know what has helped me over the years? The Lord knows all about it, and my relationship with Him has been the greatest help. The media never found out as no pictures were taken of me there with King. Terrence wanted to shelter me, and he got me out of there very quickly. Jackson apparently was not aware that I was there either, or at least for some reason he never did tell anyone. The only other people who know, of course, are Brown, my wife, you, and the demon who shot King."

Thomas continued, "This whole racial thing, will there never be a resolution to it? You and I have had extended conversations about it over the years. What is the basis for it? Why does it seem that there can be no solution?"

Angus interjected, "I remember you mentioned perhaps fear or even pride had something to do with racism, and I am sure somehow both of those are in the mix. You know the older I get, the more I see things from a spiritual vantage point."

"Preach it brother!" Thomas playfully inserted.

"You know," continued Angus, "our theology is very similar, even though you will not forgive me for being a Calvinist. We both believe in the full authority of the Bible, even though so many scholars and pastors today don't believe this. It seems that the majority of people in America believe that the Bible is an antiquated book, which if to be taken seriously needs to be reinterpreted to fit our times. But let's face it, ultimately we have to take things by faith as there are so many things not only in the Bible but also in life that we just do not fully understand. The Bible does mention strange things such as demons, angels, and sin. I remember not too long ago reading a book by the Oxford professor, C.S. Lewis, called *The Screwtape Letters*. In that book he argues that demons are real, and their goal is to cause havoc in the world. My personal view is that what is behind much of the racial unrest in this country is a spiritual component that has been largely overlooked primarily because we cannot see it. There is no way to test it in a laboratory, to perform the scientific method on it; and because of this, the majority of people, especially non-Christians, dismiss anything which suggests that there is some demonic or spiritual component to racism."

Connection

"When you think of racism in just human terms, I think what you are saying makes sense, Angus. You know that adage, 'Divide and conquer.' Could it be that somehow demons have superior intelligence, and that part of their game plan is to keep continuous divisiveness occurring among the human races?"

"I think, Thomas, that our theology says 'yes.'"

Both remained silent for some time. If one were observing them, it might appear that there were long stretches of silence. But each felt so comfortable in the presence of the other that there was no felt need to engage in continuous chatter, though both were most loquacious.

Suddenly Angus's face lit up. "Thomas, I have an idea!"

"Well, let's have it."

"What was it that caused us to be such good friends, I guess we can say, almost for a lifetime?"

"Well, that is pretty obvious. We were involved in the same activities. We started to talk to each other, even though I was somewhat reticent since you were white."

"Involved in the same activities . . . that's it!"

"Man, Angus, you are acting a little strangely."

"Thomas, both our churches are, well, filled with many who are racially prejudiced. I wager that the main reason is because they have never really been able to know someone of another race. You know that ignorance breeds fear. Just think, if you and I had just more or less stared at one another as kids and had not been open to being involved in each other's life, we probably would have continued to be aloof and somewhat suspicious of each other."

"I am not arguing against anything you have said."

The Great Journey

"Why don't we attempt to do it over again, but this time on a larger scale. We can in a sense introduce our churches to one another. Will it solve the race problem in America? No, but it is at least taking a step. Who knows where that basic step could lead? With our members praying for one another, the focus will be on our similarities and not the differences. Together both our churches represent about thirty thousand, of course not counting the television audience which we have no way of numbering. We can say with certainty though that the number is staggering."

"Angus, I don't know how many times I have heard the expression that 'from 11:00 a.m.-12:00 p.m. is the most racially segregated hour in America.'" I have heard that mainly from blacks, and the way it is said seems to be placing the blame on the entire white Christian population in America. However, I believe the fact is this is how most blacks desire the situation to remain. One thing for sure, racism certainly works both ways. Personally, I feel that whites have had to take the burden of the charge of racism, whereas I believe that the plain fact is that my people are just as racist.

Sometimes, and this may seem kind of weird, but many of my own people embarrass me with their ignorance and even superstition when it comes to white people. I almost get the impression sometimes that many blacks do not view American whites as human. I mean just think of some of the names we use such as 'honkie' and 'cracker,' and the one which always makes me cringe, 'poor white trash'. I have to admit that I still find it humorous that my people can call each other 'nigga,' but let a white do the same, and there is going to be big trouble."

"Yeah, but let's be honest about the whole issue. White America, and of course I am speaking somewhat in generalties, has not owned up to the present racism. Sure, the present generation is not responsible for the slavery of the past, but the atti-

Connection

tude which continues is deplorable. I remember one minister who tried to explain that the present racial situation is somewhat like a person who has been beaten up by a large gang. He is then rescued by a couple of powerful people who treat him very well for some time. But then as he recovers, his two would-be rescuers decide to knock him down, and then each time he attempts to pull himself up, he is tripped, slapped, poked and ridiculed. As with all illustrations, the full truth is not conveyed, but there is a good amount there."

"I am wondering why our government can't wake up," Angus blurted out as if irritated. "We can continue to talk about integration policies and implement various governmental programs, but have any of these measures brought any kind of lasting and meaningful solution? Obviously not, in fact one can probably make the case that in the past forty plus years such attempts have only caused more racial agitation. The problem as I see it, Thomas, is all these national and state governmental policies are forced; there really is no love involved. It's just kind of a trumped up humanistic-type-let-us-do-something-so-we-can-feel-good-about-ourselves thing."

"Angus, I think some of the welfare programs had their place, but it appears that the abuses gradually continued; a high percentage were abusing the system. Actually, I feel that the church should have been handling much of the problem of the poor. Without a doubt, we should have been doing more. But you are right, there has not been one American institution which has brought a solution to all that we have been talking about; this is especially the case with the government."

The conversation continued between the two until they had completely lost track of time. It would be only two months later that the plans which had been discussed were put into action.

The Great Journey

Select groups from both churches began to meet for the primary purpose of prayer. Sometimes the meetings would go on for hours. There were exchanges and common ventures between the several youth groups in each church. Middle-aged adults initiated various programs; there was much heart-felt communication taking place.

Not only were there shared programs between the two mega churches, but Angus and Thomas even arranged for a couple of Sundays when they exchanged pulpits. Needless to say, there was much controversy over that idea; both churches had a significant group who said something to the effect that maybe their pastor had better be removed; gradually, though, that controversy died in both congregations. Some of the members of both churches were not above making humorous comparisons and contrasts between the two preachers. A group from New Covenant told Angus that it would not hurt if he got a little more fire in his preaching, whereas some from Ebenezer informed Thomas that maybe he should be more intentional in pulpit demeanor. The interaction between the two churches, rather than leading to more controversy or even dying, continued to gradually escalate. Some of the members of both congregations were even going to the other church for mid-week studies or Saturday events. The various youth groups especially were involved in the exchange. One Sunday morning, Thomas had several count the number of Caucasians in attendance. He was not surprised when the total came to 550. One Sunday even more than that number of blacks were in attendance at New Covenant. Angus and Thomas began to kid each other that there were in the process of stealing the other's sheep.

Several other churches in the city began to look into the possibility of engaging in the same kind of programs, and some

Connection

of them too were successful. But the greatest impact of what was happening between New Covenant and Ebenezer was with the television audience. A high percentage of non-Christians began to tune in to the programs. The interest was high; many were saying that they never would have believed that something like this would actually be taking place in this country. A higher percentage than ever were actually showing an interest in racial issues. National media as well as such programs as *Prime Time* and *20/20* did extensive interviews of not just the two ministers, but also several of the lay people as well. Several senators and representatives, both Republican and Democrat, made impassioned speeches concerning the apparent success of what was happening. Such speeches, of course, minimized any perceived impact of the religious factors involved. Even the president of the United States in his State of the Union Address devoted a lengthy comment on the phenomenon. One interesting segment of his speech contained the words,

> ... and of course realizing the need for continued separation of church and state, I dare not comment too personally on this most successful attempt to heal past wounds. But I must admit that such success has found an astonished constituency in Washington, especially on Capitol Hill. We now are reevaluating the effectiveness of all of our attempts to bring about racial healing and equality in America. Some are saying that the spiritual element has been lacking for too long in our attempts. We implore all of you to continue to pray to God for guidance.

Some who critiqued the President's speech did indeed accuse him of crossing the line between church and state, whereas others either ignored the segment or even praised what he had to say on the subject. It was obvious that the nation was riveted to that particular segment of the annual speech. North Carolina's popular Republican senator, James Dempsey, praised the message, whereas the state's Democratic senator said that perhaps new impeachment proceedings should be initiated. He claimed that the president apparently lacked sensitivity to those of other religions, and that he must not claim only Christianity is the paradigm for healing in this country. There were only a few other voices in Congress to join him in this denunciation.

Pockets of interest, primarily in metropolitan areas, began to burgeon across America. Hundreds of the nation's largest churches gave priority attention to the new movement. Some overly positive prophets were speaking and writing about the end of racism in this country as just being over the horizon. Sociologists concluded, however, that the interest was principally among those who were under fifty years of age and was especially popular with the age thirty and under segment. Economically, the interest was primarily with the middle class. Many concluded that there appeared to be weighty emotional factors that limited the older adult's capacity to appreciate this new movement in racial harmonizing. Many preachers, priests, and rabbis began to extol the movement, and the great majority of them claimed that God was at work, and what was taking place could only be explained as supernatural. Media coverage, national and local, during 2002 predicted the end of historic racism in America.

Though the topic of racial healing had become the most popular subject in America, there was a variety of reactions. Terrence Brown and the members of the CBP viewed it as a supreme threat to their identity. The leaders had indoctrinated the members that the entire white race was evil, and that there would never be peace between the two. The idea of forgiveness was seen as asinine. Ray Rubens and the UIE emphasized that especially now the racial purity of the entire white race was in grave danger, and that the antagonism against blacks must be immediately intensified. Both Brown and Rubens primarily blamed the clergy and churches. Of course, the two names which were tossed about with utmost contempt were Angus Clark and Thomas Jackson. Many within the NAACP had a much more positive opinion of the

Connection

movement, but even this organization was divided between three factions. There was a strong alliance which claimed the whole movement was a farce; others had a wait-and-see attitude, whereas a high percentage were ecstatic about the recent occurrences.

From small-town America to metropolitan areas, there was a perceptible change in the air. Blacks and whites began to extend to one another common courtesies. Strangers were more apt to smile and make eye contact with one another. There were episodes of blacks rescuing whites, and vice versa, from burning cars and houses. But it was not the dramatic incidents as much as the sincere attention that both races, young and old, were extending to one another which became the pronounced spirit of the times.

Angus and the other leaders at New Covenant decided that the entire membership must be divided into prayer groups of twenty which would meet twice a week for an indefinite period of time for the expressed purpose of praying that the Lord would bless this new movement of His Spirit. George Padgett, a leader of one such group concluded the third month of the prayer group by praying,

> Lord, we beg your forgiveness as well as our black brothers and sisters. Lord we pray that we will have this attitude toward all races, Asians and Latinos too. We are now too painfully aware that we have not loved as you do. We have been selfish, proud, and arrogant. Somehow we have had the idea that our race and agenda are such that You are more pleased with us than with others. We have not truly heard the cries of anguish from those who have been despised for no other reason than that their difference has been seen as threatening to us. While slavery has been abolished for almost 140 years, and none of us here this evening know anything about it personally, we have been more than willing to perpetuate the antagonism. We have not been like the Good Samaritan, but we have been religious hypocrites. Lord, we believe that your

forgiveness is there for each one of us. But now help us to be determined to begin anew this relationship which we can have with all your children. Give to us grace in order that we can exude your presence, love and compassion. And if we fail, give to us the initiative to once again beg your forgiveness and to stretch out a hand of genuine compassion. This we pray in the name of our Lord. Amen.

But there were those who saw what was occurring with different eyes. And they would soon make their presence felt.

On very short notice, Rubens adjourned a meeting at his palatial home. He seemed to be somewhat frenzied as he spoke to several of the key leaders in the UIE. "I feel that it is now time to get rid of Terrence Brown. Some time ago about a dozen members paid him a visit at his shack, but we did not do too well. This time we don't want to make the same mistake."

A member daringly remarked, "You seem to have some kind of vendetta with this guy."

"All I know is that this crazy reconciliation movement seems to be working. I just can't quite get it. I bet somehow Terrence Brown is behind all of this."

The same member quipped, "Boss, this is the first time I have ever heard those words applied to you."

Seemingly ignoring the remarks, Rubens continued, "I know that Brown is somewhat tight with Thomas Jackson, that preacher. But my understanding is that Brown isn't the religious type. At this point I don't know why this fiasco of racial oneness is taking place. Looking at it from our vantage point, it would appear that Brown is the mastermind; he is always the man with the plan. We all know that preachers are in the ministry because they cannot do anything else."

Connection

Another from within the pack chuckled and remarked, "Not true, I have known several who either were on welfare or decided to give up on a failing mortician career."

"It just doesn't fit. But at this point I would wager that the real culprit is Brown. He has not only the brains and personality, but he is a master organizer."

A voice from within the pack quizzed, "What do you propose we do about it?"

"I have found out from reliable sources that Brown will be holding a fund raiser for the CBP at the Wilmington Country Club this Friday. We know that he has several cars, but for the last month he has been driving his new white Mercedes S600; I have his license plate number. There will not be valet service on that evening. Pete, I want you and Steve to be responsible for installing one of my specialties, the wam-slam-bam ignition bomb. You two are especially good at this. I have several already constructed, and at the conclusion of our time together, I will give you a couple of them for use this Friday."

It was a somewhat chilly evening. Terrence had driven over one hundred miles in order to lead the evening's activities which would be attended by four hundred prosperous individuals. The evening was going well for Terrence. "Though I don't fully agree with this new-found friendship movement that has been going on, I am most suspicious, we will continue to monitor what is happening. I don't believe we should try to stop it, at least right now. If we catch a hint of anything turning into a ploy to be used by whites for their own advantage, then we will take measures to vindicate ourselves. We know that we are most capable of doing that!"

"Look at this Mercedes! Where did he get the money for this?"

The Great Journey

"Pete, I think I see a guard coming. Hurry with that. He sure will wonder what we are doing here this evening."

"Everything is in place Steve. Let's get out of here."

"OK."

Several hundred thousand was raised that evening for the CBP. Terrence believed that the event had gone well. His audience had been most receptive to his hour-long speech, and he was gratified that those who were present encouraged his continued leadership of the CBP. Concluding his conversation with two well-known leaders, he began to walk in the light drizzle toward his car. "Mr. Brown, let me help you," said the twenty-something employee of the club. "You don't need to get yourself wet, and I would consider it a great privilege to get your car for you."

"Oh, I don't mind. For one thing it is new, just bought it a month ago, and I like driving it everywhere."

"Sir, I insist. This is even better than getting your autograph. And I'll be most careful."

"Well . . . OK, it's hard to argue with insistence."

Little did the young man know that this would be his last act of kindness. Terrence and three others at first thought that lightening had struck a car in the lot. It was not long before they viewed the carnage and instantly realized the truth.

The result of that one explosion had a rippling effect. The CBP instantly went into a defensive mode. The UIE found it incredulous that one person, Terrence Brown, could dupe them so many times. Those who were praying for peace prayed even more diligently.

5

Enemy Within

Americans were talking. and in fact the topic had become a household subject. News commentators, talk show hosts, politicians, educators, popular and academic writers, as well as numerous clergy persons were all giving forth their views on what was happening. But mainly, it was the person on the street who found the events beyond incredible. The primary question posed by many was, "Could it possibly be that the racial hatred of not just the first two years of the twenty-first century, all of the twentieth, and yes, going all the way back to 1619 when slavery was first introduced to America, be forgotten?" However, there was a curious outcry by one large segment that claimed since the differences had been going on for so long, it might be best just to let the animosities continue. A group of psychiatrists representing the American Psychiatric Association was not able to give a unified reason why they believed this reaction had occurred.

It seemed that there was no possibility to gain a consensus on why the reconcilation between the races was happening. There were many claiming that the occurrence was simply a sociological phenomenon, whereas others claimed that there was a variety of economic factors working behind the scenes. One right wing group claimed that demons were the cause. A coalition of Democratic senators claimed that the recent events simply represented "the first serious move toward racial reconciliation in America and without question is the culmination of

The Great Journey

years of promotion of civil rights and various national social programs which were initiated in the 1930s." Such explanations saw the churches involved as more of a sociological phenomenon—something that could be explained in a very logical way. Those who believed in such an interpretation claimed that other explanations, especially the religious, bordered on fanaticism since many church leaders were claiming that what was taking place was "an act of God and His Holy Spirit in the lives of men, women, and children."

Surprisingly, leaders of all three branches of Christianity—Protestantism, Roman Catholicism, and the Eastern Orthodox Church—found themselves in agreement, claiming that the movement was of God. Leaders of other religions in America such as Hinduism, Buddhism, Shinto and Confucianism simply ignored what was happening. Islamic leaders, though they would not officially endorse the movement because of various doctrinal differences, publicly announced, "What is occurring pleases Allah." The Islamic leadership did not appreciate the emphasis on Jesus Christ and the Holy Spirit; especially repelling to them was the Christian belief that Jesus was both divine and human. Key leaders within Judaism were strongly supportive. Many Rabbis, though also not acknowledging the Christian's belief of the divinity of Jesus, claimed that the movement was of God. There was much discussion between key leaders within Judaism and black America about the need for extended discussions. No Islamic leader took an active role in the movement.

A spin-off of the racial movement was the perception that there was at least the possibility for more dialogue among Protestants, Catholics, Jews, and the myriad of other religions in America. Leaders of the various sects such as Mormonism, Christian Science, and Jehovah's Witnesses did not offer a public statement concerning the recent events. But there was no mistaking the fact that this topic was big—really big. One implication that was being preached and

Enemy Within

bandied about was something called "social forgiveness and healing." To many this meant that ultimately there would be no more "isms" in America; classism, sexism, and all the others would be relegated to the ash heap of the twentieth century. Throughout 2002, from rural to suburban and urban America, the hot topic was that of the movement which had begun in Charlotte, North Carolina, when two ministers one year previously asked the question, "Why can't we introduce our people to one another?" They had no idea where in such a short period of time that question would lead.

The Grand Wizard of the United Invisible Empire continued to stare incredulously at the TV. He became physically ill and had to run to the bathroom to vomit. For months he had had to endure what he termed "the evil talk of racial oneness." He blamed what he saw as debauchery on the clergy, especially those two whom he viewed as a dastardly duo, Angus Clark and Thomas Jackson. He felt fairly comfortable that Terrence Brown also had something to do with the events of the past several months. Rubens had been briefed repeatedly in recent months concerning the activities of Brown, and there certainly was no indication that he had given up his views on the need for violence. Rubens believed that something had to be done, and quickly. He must call a meeting of his generals.

"Ladies and Gentlemen, I apologize for calling this emergency meeting of the United Invisible Empire, but we should have met sooner than this. Perhaps we could have stemmed the tide of the evil that has so engulfed us. I am convinced that instead of Terrence Brown, we should have had as our number one goal years ago the destruction of both Angus Clark and Thomas Jackson. They have caused irreparable damage to the old KKK, and they threaten to harm the unity of the UIE. I take some of the blame, but I had no idea that two

The Great Journey

preachers could cause such damage. In the past whenever we spoke of someone being a genuine danger to us, the names Malcolm X, Martin Luther King, Jr., and Terrence Brown kept surfacing. Little did I or anyone else ever imagine that there would be these diabolical two, namely Clark and Jackson, who would bring such a threat to our very existence as the superior race. Now we have everyone talking and taking seriously this new movement and its agenda. Why, even the president of the United States in his State of the Union Address devoted a lengthy segment to the sickening subject. You know where all of this is leading? There will be even more legislation and laws enacted which eventually will place blacks above whites. If it continues, the next president will be a black. Eventually all the other races that are in America will continue to have more and more rights. The gates will continue to open wider for more immigrants to come to America. The era of white supremacy has never been as threatened as it is now. Yes, comrades, we are living in the worst of times. Never in my forty years as an active member of both the KKK and UIE have I seen the situation so dismal. I have been thinking hard and long about just what we can do at this point, and I have to admit that for the first time in my long career, I have no idea what we can possibly do."

The former president of the Aryan Liberation Front, a women's supremacist group which had merged with the UIE, Sylvia Helowstein, had a suggestion. "It seems to me that we need to take our cues from these Christians or whatever they are called. If nothing else, they are apparently organized, or they can be when they want to be. I mean this movement begins with two churches, and in no time at all it spreads to other churches and even synagogues, and now we have these religious professionals with their clueless followers all talking about love, forgiveness, and racial harmony. It's absurd."

."Yeah, we're aware of all of this, so what? Do you have anything to offer which can be helpful to us?" inserted a dejected-looking member. "Not only do we have Christians, but now apparently some within Islam are saying, 'This is from God.' There are about one billion Christians in the world and close to the same number who claim Islam. Let's face it—we are dealing with a force here! Remember the One-Million-Man March! I imagine that these Christians, if they could ever really forget their differences and get together, would be able to triple that number."

A Grand Dragon assured her, "Don't get too excited, Sylvia. We all know that Christianity is very fragmented. Its members are renown for their inability to get along with one another. I imagine it is the same with the Islamic religion. And because of the war against terrorism, most Americans view all those who belong to Islam as evil."

He continued, "One thing that we must be certain we do, and that is to attempt to bring as much divisiveness as possible among all these Christians; get them fighting as much as possible among one another."

Another UIE council member quipped, "That should not be too hard. Just look at religion in America. There are all of these . . . what are they called?"

"Denominations?" suggested another.

"Yeah, that's it. I heard someone say not too long ago that there are thousands of them. One thing for sure, they don't seem to be able to get along with each other. I think we do a better job at that than they could ever do. I am not sure why there seems to be so much cooperation with this latest venture. Usually they don't cooperate on anything or at least only on a few things. Inside word is that they fight and split over such idiotic things as what kind of baptism to perform or what kind of songs should be sung. I also have heard some interesting stories about power struggles going on. Some of their best-known preachers are colorful characters, so much so that they make some of our most notorious members look somewhat tame. Remember those two guys named Jim and Jimmy back in the late 1980s?"

Lively discussion continued for several hours. Finally Sylvia hit upon an idea which captured the attention of the group. "I believe that we must attempt to infiltrate as much as possible, especially these Christian churches. We have quite a list of them, about 500 or so which are the key ones in America promoting this awful mess. We will get our people in these places, even have them join as quickly as possible so that they will actually be members. In many cases, they won't have to go to that extreme, but just our presence will cause confusion. We must organize this well. Mr. Rubens, how many members do we have?"

"At latest count, one month ago, we had close to 60,000 with about 15,000 more who though not officially members, can be counted on for anything we ask. We have certainly swelled our ranks with the addition of the other groups.

"Just think of this ladies and gentlemen," she beamed, "we have a force that can inflict the death blow to this destructive operation, and we should be able to do it without having to fire a shot. We will fight fire with fire. Divided they will fall. Without a doubt, we have the plan for massive destruction!"

The three-day session of the Directors of the United Invisible Empire, which had been called as an emergency meeting, included primarily planning on how to infiltrate key churches, including Christian and Jewish organizations, in order to cause mistrust and confusion. With intricate planning and attention to detail, the UIE's leadership finally hammered out a master plan to bring about the demise of what they saw as "the evilest plan ever devised against the white race." A quick read of the material reminded some of terrorist tactics. Anything but murder was encouraged. Of course, if one had to protect himself or

Enemy Within

herself, homicide would be justifiable. Quick dissemination of the plan to local chapters that were to hold emergency meetings assured that matters would be implemented quickly. In fact, the time frame was to be one month for all members to be notified, instructed, coached, and encouraged to select a specific plan of implementing what had been learned.

One of the associate pastors of New Covenant, Charles Griffin, excitedly inquired of Angus, "Several people who have been attending now for just a few weeks have told me many times how much they want to immediately join the church. I realize that the new member's class usually lasts for at least a month, but why don't we make an exception with these and allow them to go through the class and join in just three weeks? We can make the sessions longer than usual."

"Yes, Chuck, I have been contacted also by dozens of couples and individuals as well. As you know, I have always believed that it is not good to rush to bring in new members. It is best to try to get to know each one as much as possible. I know personally of some situations where much harm has been done by just simply trying to boost the rolls with new members. We're not a club or an organization which needs to find members in order to survive financially or attempt to impress others with numbers."

"We have never had to knock on doors in order to get new members," Chuck reminded Angus. "I remember a couple of years ago it seemed that we were besieged with requests to join New Covenant. At this time there are more in number and more of an interest to expedite the process."

The Great Journey

After much debate, Angus finally gave in to the suggestion, and he allowed three associates to instruct the potential new members. Unknown to Angus, within a three-week period of time he had taken in 153 new members of whom 71 were connected with the UIE. Not one of them had any connection with a bona fide church; the majority had actually forged what they claimed was their previous church membership, whereas the rest simply gave what Angus and the board believed was a true confession of faith. The group of 71 had been instructed for several days by a UIE member, who although not a believer, knew basic Presbyterian doctrine and the jargon of evangelical Protestantism. Usually a perceptive person, Angus was deceived by the sham; his lack of vigilance would prove most costly.

Not only Angus' and Thomas' churches were targeted, thousands of other, mid-sized to mega churches, which were promoting racial reconciliation, became the unknown subjects of the diabolical, gargantuan scheme. The attempts to cause disruption in various synagogues and Roman Catholic and Eastern Orthodox churches were not as effective. In less than three months time, the infiltration of several thousand members of the UIE into key Christian churches had occurred. A wide spectrum of churches was represented but the primary ones were Presbyterian, Methodist, Baptist, and nondenominational churches. The Grand Wizard and the Council of the United Invisible Empire had in masterful fashion implemented swiftly a program which they believed would thwart, if not reverse, the beginnings of racial healing in America.

It was not too long before Angus began to experience the results of the calculated, evil scheme. Several key Board members were coming to him disturbed over what others had been saying about the minister, the direction of the church, several board members, the church's financial accountability, and its changing image especially in Charlotte. The 71 whom Angus was responsible for admitting to the

Enemy Within

church had been very capable in the past few weeks in spreading innuendo, rumors, and lies about Angus and his wife's character. There was an especially juicy rumor about Angus' supposed sexual encounters with several women in the church. But this was only the beginning of accusations. There was an entire litany of rumors including that the whole racial agenda was just a sham to bring attention to the church and its leaders. Another most effective one was that the pastor and several key Board members were the only ones who really knew how much the annual budget was. The records said that the church was receiving about one million weekly, but according to the grapevine, the amount was considerably more, and Angus and several members of the Board were supposedly pocketing the difference.

At an emergency meeting of the staff and Board of New Covenant, the atmosphere was tense. Angus commenced, "Ladies and Gentlemen, we have been on somewhat of a roller coaster the past five or six months. We had been experiencing one blessing after another, especially that of being at the center of racial wholeness in America. Never have I seen in this church or any other the love and fullness of the Spirit that we have had until just a few weeks ago. Now it seems somehow almost overnight the whole situation has changed to one of polarization, rumors, hatred, and coldness. I am at a loss to explain what is going on here."

A member of the Board added, "It just does not make sense."

"But thinking back on how this whole movement has progressed," continued Angus, "I do remember that there were some who were almost bragging, or at least that's how it appeared to me, about what we were doing as a church for all of America. I distinctly remember that in several conversations there was no mention of what God was doing."

Several members nodded in agreement.

The Great Journey

"Also, many of the prayer groups are not meeting as often or as long as they had initially. Could it be that somehow we thought this was our work and not God's."

"Angus, there are those who are more or less saying, 'We told you so,'" offered Mary Knox. "Remember when you started the series on racial oneness years ago, and we had that little fracas right here in this room? Many are now saying that we are just reaping what was sown not too long ago."

Another member remarked, "I don't believe we have any left, at least on the Board, who are opposed to this reconciliation movement. Thad Cornelius and his little group left some time ago, thank the Lord, and my understanding is that we are now all united. Is there anyone present who disagrees with what I am saying?"

Angus, as moderator of the meeting, continued the discussion. "We have been receiving some very serious charges. I really don't feel that I need to defend myself, but I can assure you that neither Sarah nor I have been having an affair!"

"Pastor, you should not have to lower yourself by even mentioning that rubbish; we all know that there is no truth in that one," exclaimed Mark Wilson with genuine affection.

"Oh, it is not just the rumors which are bothering me. For the past few weeks now when I have stood in the pulpit to preach, the body language and facial expressions of so many people do not seem to be as receptive and warm as they were not too long ago. I find it extremely difficult to preach if I do not sense that connection with others. Some of the comments after the services have also been quite curious. I feel that I have lost my credibility with people I've known for years. We have brought so many into the church in recent months, and I do not know many of them all that well. But I'm talking about people with whom I have worked closely for years who now seem distant. At first I thought it was just in my imagination, but now I am becoming convinced that there is a real problem. I have not told any of you this until now, but I have been receiving on the average ten to twenty anonymous letters every day; most of them are filled with vindictive language. One had so many curse words, I think the author was a sailor at one time!"

Mary continued, "It just does not make sense what is going on. Just a few weeks ago, everything was almost perfect. If I were the suspicious type, I would say that some of those new people, whom we really did not get to know all that well, have something to do with the mess."

This point struck a chord with everyone in the room.

"Did anyone see the local news last night?" quizzed Mark Wilson. There is a new powerful hate group called the United Invisible Empire which has supposedly replaced the KKK. The news devoted about ten minutes to the organization. There were hundreds of them uptown Charlotte, and they were doing the usual down-with-blacks and keep-the-white-race-pure routine. They also had a lot of interesting things to say about churches which they claimed are going against what the Bible says by promoting love instead of hate between the races. One of them even mentioned New Covenant though he did not say anything about Angus personally."

Toward the end of the meeting, Angus appointed a committee of twelve to attempt to find the source of the trouble within one week. They were to be meticulous in their investigation. He was convinced that tracing rumors would lead to the source.

The Coalition of Black People held several meetings in spring 2003. As he saw and heard reports of the reversal of racial oneness, Terrence Brown, as usual, was adamant that

The Great Journey

the CBP must act and do so quickly. He had actually been quite skeptical of the reconciliation movement that had been touted for about one year as the "harbinger of the end of racial difficulties in America." Always the suspicious one, he wondered what the gimmick was. Surely, he thought, those ministers and others were into this movement only for the money, and if that were not the motive, certainly self-aggrandizement was a factor. He kept hearing from Thomas that the reason was love and forgiveness, but to Terrence those were just two meaningless words.

Of all his homes, Terrence spent most of his time at his palatial one in eastern New Jersey. He found that he was reflecting more on the meaning of his life. With middle age, he found that it was necessary to take stock of where he had been thus far in order that the remaining years would be even more meaningful. After all, his father had not lived as long as he; Terrence was painfully aware of the brevity of time. With his involvement in the CBP and the dangerous life that he led, Terrence began to realize that each day was a gift. He had repeatedly been referred to as a "maverick" by his closest friends. At first he somewhat bristled at that description, but then gradually he began to agree.

There had always been something about him that defied conventionality; maybe it was because of his legal background that he loved playing the devil's advocate. With his Harvard law degree earned with highest honors and other outward signs of success, one might be tempted to write him off as another person caught up in the American success syndrome. Not only did he belong to one of the most expensive country clubs on the East Coast, but he also owned six cars that were valued at close to one million dollars. He furnished his home only with the most expensive antiques and had a closet full of suits, each of which was purchased at a minimum of two thousand dollars; but those few who knew him realized that this too was all part of his curious psychological makeup. He did not love those "things"—that is what he called his possessions—but he acquired and gladly paraded them solely for the purpose of proving that someone of his race could make it, and do so in a big way. This was all part of his life-long plan of being the "white man's worst nightmare," the majority of whom he saw as nothing but materialistic pigs. After all, they had used the black race to attempt to build an empire, and he reasoned that his success was a direct spit in the eye, if not a low blow, to the white establishment. It felt good.

Actually, Terrence was most comfortable in his shack in North Carolina. This was the house in which he had grown to maturity. He recalled with great nostalgia the many times that he helped his father with the mules. After all these years, he still missed his dad. He was aware that he had been badly bruised emotionally by the murder of his father. He wondered what it would have been like to have grown up with him by his side, not only to comfort him during his tough teen years, but also to be head of the family. Instead, Terrence had to assume that responsibility at a young age. Though the event which took place a couple of years ago with the KKK unnerved him somewhat, he still preferred to be there over any of his other two homes. He only spent a few weeks out of each year at his home in Los Angeles, though it was not difficult to go back and forth since he had his own jet.

Terrence knew that it was time to call a meeting of the CBP. Martin Luther King, III had long abandoned the group since he believed that his affections and beliefs were more in line with the NAACP. Of course, Terrence scornfully referred to them as "that group which is happy with the status quo." The NAACP was actually larger in membership than the CBP, but in recent years had been ignored especially by the press since its agenda was not as visible and radical as was the CBP's. Terrence at first wanted to hold a big rally in

The Great Journey

Atlanta, but some of his closest advisors convinced him that there should initially be a meeting of the leadership only.

Though Terrence was aware that Thomas was not in full agreement with the CBP's position, he still decided to invite him. Picking up the telephone Thomas heard Terrence's gravelly voice, "Thomas, this is Terrence, how is everything down there in Carolina?"

"Terrence, something tells me that you are caught in New Jersey traffic, and you can hardly wait to get released," joked Thomas.

They had an unusual relationship. Being his senior by some years, Terrence considered Thomas almost as a son since he himself did not have children. Thomas considered him to be a greatly gifted person but desperately in need of God's grace, whereas Terrence viewed Thomas as a person who possessed great organizational skills but "leaned too much on the God thing." In recent months, however, Terrence's persistent questioning about the meaning and direction of his own life caused him to consider, at least momentarily, some of the things that Thomas had been telling him over the years. Terrence was very wealthy. Yet he felt empty in so many ways.

In some ways he was haunted by his Harvard education. Many blacks jeered saying that now he had the ultimate "white credential." At times he admitted to Thomas, whom he considered to be his closest friend, that he himself was "in the midst of an identity crisis."

Thomas, always patient with Terrence, continued to remind him, "You need to have God in your life in a personal way. He is the only One who can bring true meaning to you."

Terrence wandered in his thinking. He admired people like Thomas, even though he had considered them to be religious fanatics. But as he surveyed their lives, mannerisms, goals, and achievements, he began to wonder if indeed there was not something that he had missed which his keen, critical, analytical mind was not able to fully understand. He decided that at least he should keep an open mind.

"Thomas, the CBP needs to meet quickly in order to make some decisions."

"Decisions?" quizzed Thomas.

"It's obvious that the NAACP is not going to take the lead concerning the recent fiasco. I have never been able to count on them. They are so status quo. Their idea for effecting change is calling another meeting, more and more talk without any kind of action. Tell me, Thomas, what has been happening at your church?"

"There have been major disruptions, but certainly nothing like what has been occurring in most of the white churches, which leads me to guess that there has been some kind of white supremacist infiltration taking place. My good friend Angus Clark's church is on the brink of destruction; he recently told me that they now have proof that several of their new members are actually card-carrying members of the United Invisible Empire!"

The result of the meeting of the CBP was catastrophic. Meeting in Atlanta for only three days, the cadre decided that it was time to activate the revolutionary spirit. Thomas, who was only a nominal member, did not want to attend. For one thing, he believed that Terrence only invited him to add more credibility to the cause of revolution. Nevertheless, Thomas attended because he felt it was important to hear the CBP's agenda for himself.

The Great Journey

During the first two days, Thomas heard the whole litany of injustices inflicted upon the black race by supposed evil whites and their system. The speeches were passionate, especially those which detailed the loss of life on the Atlantic during the slave trading years. He heard several claim that the only reason blacks were introduced to Christianity was to manipulate slaves, the goal being to make them more docile and subservient to their white masters.

When Thomas protested that they were citing too much history and not dealing with the present, there was an en mass protest that the new racism is the glass ceiling that is every bit as constricting as the old slavery. He even heard several talk about "Uncle Toms." He knew most were speaking directly to him.

Thomas had forcefully argued for abandoning any idea of initiating a revolution, but his was the only voice for moderation among the group of twenty-five. His impassioned speech included such attempts of persuasion as, "Why do you blame all of white America? What you are saying and planning is not even logical. It took two races to build America. Oh yes, we were the slaves for about 250 years, but we have the same freedoms today as the white race. Black people have more privileges in America than in any other country, so why would anyone advocate destruction? If nothing else, we are only hurting all black people."

Not one of the other twenty-four disputed him, but Thomas knew that his message was not registering with them. Their lack of eye contact and shaking of their heads were not subtle clues that he had failed to convince them.

Not to be discouraged, he continued, "Have any of you ever even tried to befriend a white person, or have you always engaged in the usual non-thinking routine of bad-mouthing? I know we all hate that phrase on the part of whites, 'one of my best friends is black,' which we think seems to be somewhat insincere. But when I say that one of my best friends, if not my best friend, is white, I am being completely sincere. I chose to be friends with him, and we have been close friends for many years. I have a strong suspicion that not one of you has ever even thought of doing likewise. So you continue on with your rage at a nebulous white opponent. Every white person alive today did not have a thing to do with slavery, yet most of us treat them as if they did. Your behavior actually seems quite childish to me."

Tyrone Washington, a big, burley man snapped, "I think we have heard enough of you and your meanderings! Let's move on to someone who has something of substance to say."

Thomas knew that he had come to an impasse, and not even Terrence rose in his defense. Finally he realized that there might as well be 10,000 miles of distance between himself and Terrence. Though they had shared so much from the past, spiritually Thomas realized that they were light years apart. He liked Terrence and was quick to admit that he admired his wit, intelligence, leadership skills, and courage. But his total lack of God-awareness expressed itself in a profound self-absorption.

The outcome of the meeting was that the CBP recommended the revolution begin, especially pinpointing members of the United Invisible Empire. Thomas's message, not to judge the whole by the few, fell on deaf ears. All points of black power were to be utilized. To be targeted was every major metropolitan area in America. Political leaders, from governors to mayors, were to be enlisted. Preachers were to proclaim the gospel of civil disobedience. Attempts were to be made in order to recruit the majority of members of the NAACP, though it was known that the leadership of the organization would not support the CBP's agenda. Leaders for every locality were identified. Force was to be encouraged from the national to the

The Great Journey

grass roots level. And the special targets were to be members of the UIE.

The United Invisible Empire was invisible no longer. Reminiscent of the marches of the nineteenth and early twentieth centuries, parading members made their presence known in cities, small and large, across America. The infiltration of major churches continued. Of course, the media followed their every move. Interviewing Ray Rubens on May 8, 2003, CNN asked him several leading questions about the direction and goals of the UIE. Watching the interview, Thomas studied the face more closely—the person being questioned looked strangely familiar to him, but he just could not place where and when he had seen him before. For some strange reason, as he looked at Ray Rubens on television, Thomas began to feel great fear, agitation, and a sickening sensation. He had never had such an experience. He reasoned either he somehow knew this person or Rubens reminded him of someone else for whom he held a great antipathy.

Rubens's interview was memorable. He made such statements as, "As head of the United Invisible Empire, I and my followers are committed to an America that our forefathers envisioned. America is the true home of only those who are of white blood. We have had it with this Coalition of Black People. They have no claims upon this country, and it is our purpose to see that they are finally put in their place. We are now a force of such magnitude that any group, including the military will have a tough time dealing with us. If the CBP does not cease its threat of terrorist tactics, we will be forced to subdue them."

"But Mr. Rubens, don't you think that you are overstating matters?" the reporter asked as if half amused.

Enemy Within

She continued, "In this day of political correctness, don't you think your movement represents something from an era long ago?"

"We are serious, dead serious. These people are getting much too uppity. We never should have given in to them way back in the 1950s and again all through the sixties. The KKK was around then, but now my organization is much stronger. We shall overcome!"

Thomas and Angus had been in constant communication for the past month. Both instinctively knew that events would only escalate to a full-scale civil war if something did not happen soon to prevent such an episode. Both their churches were suffering; Angus's ministry was in a desperate decline because of the internal conflicts that continued at machine-gun rapidity.

Thomas had been having recurring nightmares, something that he had never experienced before. The most common one was of a huge, ugly face chasing him. In his dream, he knew that he had to run fast or else he would be devoured.

"Thomas, how did it all get so crazy?"

"I don't think that there is only one reason."

"Just a few months ago, Thomas, all of America was talking about healing and love, not the differences but the similarities. Without question, the UIE has been most effective in attempting to destroy what God was allowing us to accomplish."

"Angus, we both are very aware that this is primarily a spiritual battle. Those who follow our ministries know this. I have to admit that sometimes I must confess the ways of God confuse me. We say that He is omnipotent and present everywhere, but if this really is the case, why can evil be so powerful? It does appear at times that evil is stronger, and if that is true, the God we serve is limited. Notice I am not saying that this is my conclusion, but I will say that I am struggling with this."

"The infiltration of our churches, especially New Covenant, has been most effective on their part. Ray Rubens is something; I don't imagine too many people would want to be in the same room with him. He does look wicked."

As if in a daze, Thomas suddenly cried out, "Oh no! It can't be true!"

"What Thomas?"

"It's him! That face. I knew that I recognized it from somewhere in the past. Ray Rubens is the face from April 1968. He's the one who shot Martin Luther King! That image has been with me for thirty-five years."

"I have always known that you have a great memory, but aren't you maybe overdoing it a little?"

"Angus, that face has been with me for years. He even combs that thick wavy hair the same way, only now it is gray. But one of the main tip offs is the big, obvious scar across his chin. I have never been more convinced."

"Did Terrence see him?"

"Not really. He did catch a glimpse of a figure moving away from the window. He thought that he saw some kind of object. It could have been a gun, but he just was not sure. No one else on the balcony or below saw anything. It has been a curse that I am the only one who could identify him. Remember, I was never even questioned. Terrence made sure that I would not be brought into the whole mess."

"It is hard to know what to do," continued Angus. "We can bring accusations, but what good will it do. It is apparent that the country is on the verge of anarchy. It probably would take years even before a trial could begin. As of now, you are the only witness. It would be your word against his. Then there would be all the questioning about why you never came forward and told anyone that you were there. Of course, we both know it is the difference between day and night when it comes to your character and Ray Rubens's, but many times the legal system does not acknowledge that."

"Maybe the next best thing we can do is have a meeting with Rubens. Thomas, I will try to contact him and arrange a meeting. I doubt if he will come if there is anyone else but me."

"Angus, what good will it do for you to confront him? What do you expect him to do, confess and ask for forgiveness!"

"What else can we do? Our country is embattled over racism. Who knows what will be remaining of our cities or our country in a month or so? I know that you would like to meet with him, confront him, but let me do that."

"Why shouldn't I be there as well?"

"Thomas, it just would not work. Maybe we can do it this way. I'll let you know where I am going to meet with Rubens. You do what you want. Even though Rubens is worse than unethical, I am not going to lie to him when I say that I am the only one who will be meeting with him. I'll tell you the place and time, but Thomas I'm not inviting you. You are only being informed."

The Trial

The friction between the UIE and the CBP continued to escalate. Other ethnic groups became more vocal and there was further polarization. It seemed that America was no longer, "one nation under God, indivisible," but was now very much fragmented. Asian-Americans, Latinos, American Indians, and other minority groups all began to clamor about various injustices and their rights. Some Arab-Americans were preaching about Jihad and a Muslim holy war. But none had any official organization or any collective plans for retaliation. Each group had what they considered to be a major grievance against whites in general and the government in particular.

Across America, primarily in metropolitan areas but also in suburban and rural communities, gunfights were breaking out, and in some cases, hundreds were involved. In many situations, the fights were more like battlefields, particularly when heavy weapons were used. Large explosions were common in such cities as Los Angeles, Chicago, St. Louis, Dallas, Detroit, Minneapolis, Boston, Birmingham, Columbus, and Atlanta. The rumor was that all major buildings would come to the same fate as the Twin Towers in New York City. The NAACP made an official comment on the situation, but remained, on the whole, estranged from the conflict. Curiously, in many situations, the police and the National Guard did not intervene, even when explosives were used. There was no denying that the country was now in desperate trouble. News commentators made statements such as, "The racial riots of the 1960s were only a prelude to what is happening now." The phrase, "The Second Revolution," was a common one, especially among devotees of the CBP.

Angus somehow managed to carry on the daily responsibilities of ministry, but he found his sermon preparation and delivery especially difficult. "What was he to say?" he pondered. He could sense the uneasiness of the dwindling congregation on Sunday mornings. Invariably, there were rude comments or many that he interpreted as double-entendres. Though those who had known him for a long time, and especially his family, defended him, he knew that many no longer supported him or the ministry at New Covenant, not to mention the radio and television audiences. He had spent a lengthy time on the issue of racism, and for several months it seemed that a miracle had occurred; but now "Lord, what a mess," he mused. And those rumors, what was he to do, go public and denounce every one of them? Or if he did, would some assume that he was guilty because addressing the issue might be perceived as nothing more than an attempt to justify himself?

Twelve members of the United Invisible Empire had been identified at New Covenant. Angus felt betrayed. Never would he have imagined that such nice, refined-looking people were actually members of a notorious white supremacist hate group, which ultimately was responsible for the mayhem not only in his church but throughout the country. He persistently asked himself, how he could have been duped so easily. The twelve who had been identified seemed so sincere. He even remembered that three in particular excelled in their knowledge and zeal for matters pertaining to the Christian faith. Their testimonies on the whole seemed genuine to him. As Angus reflected on the past few months, he remembered that about the time that large group was brought into membership, he had been

The Trial

somewhat lax in his personal spiritual walk. He had been merely composing sermons rather than meditating. Caught up in all the excitement, he had neglected his own spiritual needs. Was it possible that there was also a hint of pride? He was aware that the Bible had a great deal to say about this hideous sin. His prayer life had been somewhat remiss as well. It dawned on him that he had lacked perception because he himself was not as strong as he should have been. The shepherd had been nodding while the wolves gained entrance into the fold. He determined that never again would this happen.

There was no reason why any of them should be of help in his attempt to contact Ray Rubens. After all, they had simply used him, Angus reasoned, and they had no real affection for him. His first four attempts to locate the whereabouts of Rubens met with a mixture of defiance and embarrassment because Angus had discovered them. But his fifth attempt, Steve Norris, a thirty-something man, offered help.

"Dr. Clark, I know that I have used you . . . and, well I just don't want to talk anymore about the subject."

"I am not here to condemn you or anyone else who is part of the UIE, though I must say that you duped me completely. All I want to do is contact Ray Rubens. Can you at least help me with this?"

"Yes, but on one condition."

"I think I already know what that is."

"You must not tell him how you found out where to locate him."

"Are you afraid of him?"

"Yes and no. He has a power about him that I have never seen in another person. He can appear enticing and dangerous simultaneously. He has this way of getting you to do things that you would not even think about engaging in for another person. Some have said he has demons. Others just talk about his charisma. I would literally be afraid for my life if he knew that I gave you any information. I have heard talk about what happened to two or three who double-crossed him. We are sworn to secrecy."

Through much adroitness, Angus was able to make contact with Ray Rubens and set a place and time for a meeting. One lead led to another. Initially, he was told that Rubens did not have a telephone, but he was able to acquire the number. After an initial short conversation, they agreed to communicate by e-mail. Several cites were suggested between Eastern North Carolina and Charlotte such as Salisbury, Pinehurst, or even Rubens's primary residence in Mayfield. Finally, Rubens agreed to meet with Angus two days later in a reserved room at the Adam's Mark Hotel in Greensboro at 9:00 p.m. on June 28, 2003.

But he issued a solemn warning to him, "Don't try anything funny. I have plenty of people who are watching out for me."

Almost immediately Angus experienced a great sense of foreboding. One thing for sure, no one would accuse him of timidity, but he was now experiencing a fear as he never had known before. He knew that he would be facing evil incarnate. He envisioned all the forces of hell being unleashed upon him. He wondered if he would be strong enough. Was there some niche in his spiritual armor that would prove to be his Achilles' heel? Images of marching Klansmen from the past continued reverberating through his soul. The horrors of what one race had inflicted upon another effortlessly burst to the surface of his mind. The cross burnings, lynchings, rapings, lootings, and a myriad of other atrocities loomed before him as if actually being witnessed. Angus knew that he must talk with Thomas.

The Trial

"Watch your back," warned Thomas. "Why don't you at least take a hidden recorder so you can make sure that the conversation is remembered accurately just in case in the future Rubens tries to use anything against you?"

"I gave him my word that there would be no witnesses, weapons, or recorders."

"Angus, I just have a bad feeling about this. This meeting could be way beyond you, or me for that matter. Did he ask you why you wanted to meet with him?"

"Yes, and I said simply that I wanted to hear from him about the direction of the revolution. He knows about my association with you, but he did not ask much about that. I believe that he thinks I want to strike some kind of deal with him. He apparently does know that my church isn't going to be around much longer. He probably thinks that I am desperate and will do anything that he says."

"Angus, I need to be there with you. You don't really know what this guy is capable of. He may either have some hit men waiting for you, or he may just have plans to do it himself as he did with King."

"I learned long ago to have no fear of anyone but God alone."

"I know what you are saying, but sometimes I wonder about your common sense. Is it OK if I go with you?"

"No, Thomas, I am not inviting you to come. Please don't ask me again. You know the place, date, and time."

The Great Journey

Angus continued in prayer until early in the morning of the day of their scheduled meeting. He asked the Lord to protect him. He requested that he would be strong spiritually, and physically if needed.

Arriving at 8:45 p.m. at the Adam's Mark, Angus was escorted to the third floor, down a long dimly lighted corridor, and to a small conference room. The room was posh; a large mahogany conference table graced the room. Poring himself a glass of ice water, Angus waited. The former fear attempted to surface again, and he caught himself thinking that it was foolish for him to be here waiting for a person whom he thought was demon-possessed. The large grandfather clock told him he had five minutes. He could still leave and perhaps not be recognized since he and Rubens had never met in person. He began to perspire as if he had been exercising vigorously for a considerable period of time.

The next two minutes seemed to be like an eternity. Then he was aware of someone's presence in the room, and standing over him. Angus pushed back his chair, and steadily rose until their eyes locked. Each was to be surprised. Rubens felt a strange recoil in his soul. Never had he seen such pristine, penetrating blue eyes, the kind of gaze which makes one feel that the beholder knows all about you—knows you better than you even know yourself. Angus did not feel any fear. Instead, Angus sensed reticence and even apprehension in Rubens.

There were no pleasantries exchanged. Angus, a master of perceiving human emotions, charged, "I know all about you, Ray. I know that you killed Martin Luther King, Jr."

"Is this the only reason why you have taken my valuable time? Even if your ridiculous charge were true, guess what? There is no way in hell you can prove it."

For the next minute not a word was said. The test of wills was becoming even more intense. Though Angus knew he

The Trial

should be fearful, for some reason he felt courage. He was not naïve enough though not to realize that his life possibly was in grave danger.

Rubens was the first to break the silence with the question posed with a sneer, "So, what kind of game are you up to now?"

"I am not a person of games."

The prolonged silence continued.

The two men jolted when both Terrence and Thomas flung open the door and moved quickly toward Rubens. Without saying a word, Terrence quickly positioned himself behind Rubens and grabbed him around the neck in a hold that could instantly break his neck.

"Where are my guards?" rasped Rubens.

"Terrence, I did not know you were going to do this!" shouted Thomas. "You promised me that we would just talk with him."

"I'm talking!" muttered Terrence.

"Don't kill him, Terrence," pleaded Angus. "This is exactly why I did not want you to come. Thomas, didn't I tell you that you were not invited? How did you get past the guards?"

"Terrence decided to use some of his Green Beret tactics. You did give me all the details, and you did not say specifically that I should not come."

Rubens's eyes were beginning to bulge out from his crimson face. He had the unmistakable look of terror stamped on him. For the first time in his life he began to have feelings of remorse. Before him flashed the many murders and other atrocities in which he had been involved. He was experiencing psychological hell because he now realized that he was guilty—and caught.

"Terrence, don't lower yourself to his level," Angus pleaded in a deliberate, halting tone. "Let the highest court take care of him."

"Oh no, here we go again with the God thing. Why should this piece of slime be allowed to live. Please don't start quoting the Bible and all that forgiveness trash. I think I could kill him right now, and even an all-white jury would acquit me. You are looking at the face of one Ray Rubens, a vile person who has caused more tragedy and heartbreak than anyone else living or dead in America. He's the killer of not only King, but countless others. He destroyed our country a long time ago and is intent on making matters even worse."

Thomas attempted to convince Terrence with all the persuasive powers he possessed to spare Rubens's life. After almost a half-hour, he gradually released the death hold he had on him. Rubens was only semi-conscious.

After reviving him, they spent three hours in an intense dialogue attempting to find out more information from Rubens. Finally, he admitted that he murdered Martin Luther King, but begged that his life be spared. The once arrogant, self-sufficient man was now groveling for mercy. To the three he actually seemed somewhat pathetic; even Terrence felt this emotion.

Finally it was Angus who, with a touch of humor, suggested, "Let's now have a trial. I'm sure that Mr. Rubens is most familiar with this kind. Let's see, I believe that it is called a mock trial. Terrence, you be both judge and jury. Thomas, you are the defense attorney, and I am the one responsible to prosecute him."

The next two hours passed fairly quickly for the three, but for Rubens it was the longest 120 minutes of his life. Rubens

The Trial

thought this was a literal trial. He had not seen the wink from Angus to the others. The three realized that because of the current conditions of the country, years might pass before Rubens would be tried, if ever. Their duty, they reasoned, was to at least be able to teach him a huge taste of what he had inflicted upon others They believed that they had an even better method than physical violence.

Angus set the rules. "Normally, the prosecution goes first, but we will do this trial backwards. I am sure that Mr. Rubens will not mind. We will save the prosecution to the last."

"Attorney Jackson, present your case," commenced Terrence.

"Your honor and jury, this man is the by-product of a bad environment. He just cannot help but being the kind of person he is. I know for a fact that he grew up in a sordid environment. Why there is even good evidence that there was a Confederate flag in every room of his childhood house. We believe that his parents never did have anything good to say about black people. Then, of course your honor and jury, there are the debilitating genetic factors. It is obvious that his inherited traits are such that he is predisposed to racial bigotry. Your honor in other words, he just can't help it."

"Objection, your honor, the defense attorney has no credible evidence for these statements," shouted Angus.

"Objection overruled," retorted "Judge" Terrence.

"Your honor, surely it is reasonable that both environment and genetics play key roles in the psycho-pathology of my client. Granted he should have been placed in a state mental institution many years ago, but the system failed him. I don't believe that there is a facility in the world which will be able to rehabilitate him—he is so pathetic and far gone."

The Great Journey

Rubens did not say a word, but stared straight ahead with a glassy look in his eyes.

"Further, your honor, getting back to the Confederate flag issue. Imagine, if you can, what it would be like to view such a flag, day after day, from early childhood to adulthood. I believe that as he looked at the flag, it became part of his psyche; yes, the warping began early on for him. Without a doubt those Confederate flags in his home at that impressionable age led to his racist attitude—his hatred of the black race.

He gradually began to connive a plan on how he could torment the entire race. He even had murderous thoughts beginning at this early period in his life."

"Objection your honor. We don't know how many confederate flags were in his home. Also, the phrase, "murderous thoughts" claims the defendant was and is capable of thinking for himself."

"Objection sustained."

"Look again, your honor and jury, at the genetic issue. We believe it is now possible to isolate a particular gene called 'the bigotry impulse gene.' Through careful research, we have now discovered that many suffer with this. The preponderance of those who have this malady live below the Mason-Dixon Line, though there is evidence that many above the line suffer from this aberration as well. Your honor and jury, so many others have never been implicated who have this problem. No, they are free. Why and how can we possibly accuse this poor victim? Also, let me say this concluding thought on the genetic issue. Another gene has been isolated. At first we thought it was another type of the bigotry impulse gene, but through most careful analysis, we now know this is a distinct gene. Remember it is very close, but there is a shade of difference, and that is why we call it 'the black bigotry impulse gene.' Most scientists agree that it

The Trial

is manifested mainly in certain redneck-type behavior, but curiously only a fairly small percentage of the redneck class express this anti-black behavior. So, it could be that even more research is needed. But I hope you are able to see how forceful an argument this is.

"Finally, your honor and jury, there is the issue of the scar. Ultimately we just don't know the source of it. But there is a rumor that it happened when the defendant became enamored with a black woman and holding her closely, he attempted to kiss her. Little did he know that she thought he was trying to force her. She grabbed whatever she could in order to defend herself, in this case a box opener, and let him have it right across the chin. So you see, jury and your honor, this is further proof of the psycho-pathology of my client. Every day for years and years whenever he looked in the mirror, he was reminded of the day he tried to kiss a black lady. Your honor, he has to admit daily that he was jilted by this lady."

"Objection, your honor, there is no evidence that the defendant did not actually kiss the black lady."

"Objection sustained."

"In closing, jury and your honor, I recommend leniency for my client. If you decide that he should die for his crimes, I recommend that we do it immediately after our trial. I suggest, if you have not believed my impassioned defense, that he be brought to an out-of-the-way place outside the city and there be hanged from a tree. Now if for some reason you don't prefer this method, I suggest death by a high powered rifle, one clean shot to the head. Certainly this is a method with which he is most familiar. But of course, I trust that you will accept my cogent defense. When you combine all three, the confederate flag theory, his genetic makeup, and of course, the lady, there is no doubt that he should be exonerated."

The Great Journey

It was obvious that Rubens, his face no longer red but white, could not take anymore. "If you don't let me out of here, I am going to start shouting as loud as I can. Don't you think that someone is going to hear me?"

Answering swiftly, Terrence convinced him to keep quiet. "I dare you to do that, and I'll be over there in no time with another hold around your neck, and this time you will really be red-faced."

Terrence continued, "And now we have the certain prosecution of the defendant. Attorney Clark, present your case."

"Your honor and member of the jury, I have heard some powerful arguments concerning the solid character of Mr. Rubens. But I believe that I can prosecute best by using the very arguments of the defense. First the environmental argument is an important one. Mr. Rubens grew up in a home where guns were used. Careful investigation has confirmed this fact. He became a crack shot at an early age, but the targets were rabbits and raccoons. We have substantial evidence that this is what happened. At the age of fourteen, he heard some of his friends say that they were going 'coon hunting,' and of course he thought that they meant raccoon; little did he know that they were talking about black people. So yes, he was initially led astray by his family and friends, but he certainly knew better by this age. Yes, he is accountable for his actions. He simply found this new type of hunting much more exciting. There you have the motive. It was purely the thrill of the hunt, your honor and jury."

"Objection, your honor. The prosecuting attorney seems to be saying that my client does indeed know right from wrong."

"Objection sustained."

"There is next, your honor and jury, the issue of genetics. Mr. Rubens has even duped his own attorney. Latest careful

The Trial

research has definitively proven that the black-bigotry impulse gene is not inherited. Strangely, it shows up in a person's genetic code after a prolonged period of having murderous thoughts and literally engaging in murder against black people. Again, just like the environmental argument, the conclusion is that he himself decided in both cases; therefore, he is guilty by virtue of the fact that he had a choice between right and wrong, and he chose the wrong."

"Objection, your honor, prosecution implies that my client is capable of duping anyone."

"Objection sustained."

"Finally, concerning the scar theory, and I remind you that this is another attempt by the defense to cover up the facts. There were actually two black women he was chasing. Notice, he was literally chasing them! He could not resist them. What happened was he somehow was able to catch them, and both were afraid of being forced. One of the two then used a knife that fell out of his shirt pocket to cut him across the chin. But you might be thinking, 'OK, that's nice, but what about the scar?' He was actually very proud of the scar. It reminded him of the day he caught two black ladies and lived to tell about it."

"Your honor and jury, this concludes my prosecution of Mr. Rubens."

"I thank both defense and prosecution for their arduous efforts. You both have presented many cogent arguments, and as foreman of the jury I know that we could be in recess ad infinitum. But I believe we have heard enough to make an expeditious conclusion. We find the defendant guilty by reason of choice. He is to be sentenced to death by firing squad within three hours."

The atmosphere again became serious. The three believed that Rubens had been subjected to something worse than a thrashing; he had never experienced that kind of ridicule before, and the look on his face revealed that fact. During much of the mock trial, he forcefully placed his right hand over his left chest as if he were having heart problems. He did not look any of the three in the eyes, but looked slightly above their heads. He believed that soon the three would kill him; terror gripped him because he hadn't realized that the trial had been done in jest—although totally at his expense.

Two night clerks, making quick use of a key, gained entrance into the room. In the confusion of their entrance, Rubens immediately saw his chance, and in a flash he disappeared along with the two body guards who had regained consciousness and managed to untie themselves. In their retreat one brandished a large caliber pistol threateningly aimed at the three.

The destruction continued. Gun battles raged in most of the larger cities in America. The decimation of large inner city buildings became commonplace. Because most police departments were divided along racial lines, they were not effective and in many instances actually proved to be a hindrance. Even the National Guard in many areas was not able to stop the destruction. Desperate, the president announced that the armed forces, in particular the Marines, were the last hope for saving the country.

Seven days after Angus and Thomas had met with Ray Rubens, they found themselves in the sanctuary of the Ebenezer Baptist Church. The bright lights focusing on the large cross seemed to have a green hue to them.

"Thomas, there apparently are some people who give themselves over to evil for so long that they seem to be beyond

The Trial

hope. Sometimes I wonder if Ray Rubens is outside the reach of the Lord. We don't know where he is. We don't know what he will do next, where he will show up again. But Terrence is perhaps a different story."

"I agree. In recent weeks he has been asking me all kinds of questions about religion and the Bible. It's as if he is really interested and not trying to debate everything. He seems to be genuinely searching. I believe that there is hope for him."

"Angus, somehow along the way we left God out of the equation. We started well; people all over the country were praying and seeking God's guidance. But then we began to believe that we were the architects of what had been taking place. Let's start over.

.Looking searchingly into the eyes of Thomas, Angus said with hope, "For several months not long ago there was peace and oneness. I believe that it can happen again."

About the Author

Jeffrey Jon Richards holds master's degrees from Dallas Theological Seminary and Drew University. He received a Ph.D. in systematic theology from Drew University. He has also done post-doctoral work at Oxford (England), Marburg and Tübingen (Germany). He is an ordained Presbyterian minister and has pastored several churches. He also taught for many years as a visiting professor at the University of North Carolina-Charlotte and has taught at several seminaries.